Three Against One . . .

Joshua Strongheart said, "Listen, I am a Pinkerton agent and can show you all my badge and credentials."

Luke Blackwell, whose family owned a plantation along the Peedee in the Sandhills of North Carolina, said, "I don't care what lie you wanna yarn. We found yer moccasin tracks outside our mine last night, an dey was leadin' away our horses. Dane, git a rope."

The one to Blackwell's right started to take a step, and that was exactly what Joshua needed. The half-breed's hand whipped down to his Colt .45 Peacemaker, brought it out cocked, and fired. Flame stabbed from the barrel, and a big red spot on Dane's rib cage appeared as he folded like a suitcase. Strongheart's left hand fanned the hammer, and flame stabbed out again, and a bright red spot appeared in the middle of Luke's nose and the back of his head literally exploded. Strongheart's left hand fanned the hammer again, and that shot hit the left one, Foster, in the stomach a split second after he fired the bullet kicking up dirt between Strongheart's legs. The three bullets had been fired in less than a second, but the third did not hit the man squarely in the stomach, and Joshua fanned the hammer again and shot Foster again, dead center in the chest. He swayed and fell forward on his face, very dead.

THE RIDER
OF PHANTOM
CANYON

Don Bendell

BERKLEY
New York

BERKLEY
An imprint of Penguin Random House LLC
375 Hudson Street, New York, New York 10014

Copyright © 2016 by Don Bendell
Penguin Random House supports copyright. Copyright fuels creativity, encourages
diverse voices, promotes free speech, and creates a vibrant culture. Thank you for buying
an authorized edition of this book and for complying with copyright laws by not
reproducing, scanning, or distributing any part of it in any form without permission.
You are supporting writers and allowing Penguin Random House to continue to
publish books for every reader.

BERKLEY is a registered trademark and the B colophon is a trademark of
Penguin Random House LLC.

ISBN: 9780425266564

First Edition: October 2016

Printed in the United States of America
1   3   5   7   9   10   8   6   4   2

Cover art by Bruce Emmett
Cover design by Lesley Worrell

It is far harder to kill a phantom than a reality.

—Virginia Woolf

The character Joshua Strongheart is a true American hero that I have created, and this is the fourth and final book in the series. It is only appropriate that I dedicate this book to three very important heroes whom I truly love and who have played major roles in my own personal life. While writing this book, I went through a heartbreaking issue barely two years after losing my soul mate and wife of thirty-two and a half years, Shirley Bendell, whom I dedicated *The Indian Ring* to. I had several friends comforting me, but one friend truly helped me daily through the process, because she has been through so much trial by fire herself, and on an international stage, and emerged a major hero in more ways than one. She was personally honored as "a true national hero" by then-President George W. Bush, and she has been vilified by liberal media pundits and gossiped about by many of those whom she made look like fools. Jeanne Assam is a very close and trusted friend and confidant of mine. She is the courageous police officer who was forced by circumstance to engage in a shootout with serial killer Matthew Murray, the gunman who entered New Life Church in Colorado Springs on December 9, 2007, and opened fire on innocent, screaming churchgoers after he had already shot and killed four people near Denver, killing two and wounding two others. After sending an email warning and armed with numerous weapons and thousands of rounds of ammunition, Murray drove an hour south to New Life Church in Colorado Springs, where he killed two sisters and wounded their father and another in the parking lot. Then, he entered the church with seven thousand people at the service and opened fire inside. He was shooting a semiautomatic rifle with rounds spewing out as fast as he could pull the trigger. Jeanne, who was going to stay home while praying and fasting for several days, but felt "strongly inspired" that day to go to church, where she volunteered as a security officer, held fast in a hallway while others ran screaming. Jeanne prayed, then gave him a chance to lay down his weapons. He fired wildly. She was the only officer there who did not know that Matthew Murray had emailed and warned the church leadership he was coming to kill more, and that the Colorado Springs police were warned he was coming. They'd beefed up security, but he waited until some off-duty officers left. Jeanne did not run screaming. She never runs with the flock. Jeanne was, and is, a sheepdog, a professional police officer whose goal was always to serve and protect others. He could kill or wound no more, because armed only with a trust in God, the raw courage of a true warrior, and a 9mm pistol, she ran into Murray's withering rifle fire, shooting back at him with very accurate fire while moving forward at him, and hit him ten times with her own bullets, the last from only five feet away, killing him, saving countless lives, and she was covered with his arterial blood. Not only is Jeanne one of my heroes, and a true, genuine law enforcement professional, she is a very close and trusted friend who was solidly there for me at a very critical and painful time in my life. That negative situation turned into a positive for me anyway, but could have been worse had Jeanne not been there uplifting me. Thank you, Jeanne. I love you very much, my beautiful friend.

The second person I honor herein is another of my heroes and a man with only one name, Ek—a name that means "manure." A native belief was to give men such names to ward off evil spirits from the jungle. In 1968 and 1969, when I served in South Vietnam as a young U.S. Army Special Forces (Green Beret) first lieutenant, I lived with, trained, and fought alongside the Vietnam War's toughest fighters: the aboriginal nomadic Montagnard tribespeople. I lived with the Jeh tribe at a very remote place along the Laotian border called Dak Pek. Having a Montagnard lover, as well as a seven-year-old orphan named Plar whom I wanted to adopt, but who was raped and murdered by the Vietnamese, I developed a very close relationship and strong bond with the "Yards." In short order, they assigned six bodyguards to me, who shadowed me everywhere that I went day and night. It was a great honor among them to be a bodyguard for me, because I was an American, and they were each supposed to die before I would. They called me "Trung-uy (First Lieutenant) Cowboy." One of those bodyguards was a delightful, muscular little man named

Dedication

Ek, who had five sons who fought for us, and a nephew who was also one of my bodyguards. In late summer of 1968, after our sister Special Forces A camp of Dak Seang came under siege, I commanded a 160-man joint operation with one hundred Montagnard strikers (mercenaries) from Dak Pek and sixty from Dak Seang. I was joined by two fellow Green Berets, who were sergeants. Dak Seang had been under siege and attack for days by a regiment of highly trained, well-equipped NVA (North Vietnamese Army) regulars. We got into a major battle west of Dak Seang, and I was wounded, with my right wrist bandaged up, unusable, and in an expedient sling. I was firing my own weapon left-handed, was directing a counterattack, and was also on the radio directing mortar, artillery fire, and, later, tactical air strikes onto the enemy positions. During the height of the battle, when NVA sprang a spider hole ambush with American Claymore mines and automatic weapons at point-blank range, Ek immediately ran in front of me to shield and protect me and was shot three times by an AK-47 and blasted by an American Claymore mine that literally blew the canteen off my hip, tore my camouflage tiger suit all over, and sent me flying backward onto my back. Ek took the whole blast in his legs and torso. I ended up giving mouth-to-mouth resuscitation to the dying man while left-handed, while also administering IVs into each arm with serum albumin, a blood expander. He died as the skids of the medevac helicopter touched down. His large, muscular nephew, another one of my bodyguards, had Claymore pellets in his shins and had his left eye shot out. I took my black cowboy kerchief and bandaged his eye and stuck and lit a cigar in his mouth during the fight. Ignoring his wounds, he bent over, picked up Ek, and proudly placed his uncle's body on the dustoff chopper, and then argued with me as I made him get on the medevac, too. He wanted to stay and guard me.

Right before Ek died, he looked up at me, smiling with yellow teeth, and weakly said, "Me go see Jesus now."

Choking back tears, I said, "I will take care of your family. Tell Jesus I said hi."

Thank you for saving my life, Ek. I love you.

Green Beret Colonel Roger Donlon, MOH, was the very first recipient of the Congressional Medal of Honor in the Vietnam War. On July 6, 1964, then-Captain Roger Donlon was serving as the commanding officer of the U.S. Army Special Forces Detachment A-726 at Camp Nam Dong when a reinforced Viet Cong battalion suddenly launched a full-scale, predawn attack on the camp. The battle lasted five hours, and during the battle Roger was wounded many times, yet crawled from position to position, dragging wounded men from bunkers, carrying ammunition and weapons to defenders, administering first aid, and continually exposing himself to enemy fire while doing so. He kept getting wounded in the face, arms, legs, and abdomen but would not stop and take care of himself, only of his men. By daylight, the Viet Cong were defeated and retreated into the jungle, leaving fifty-four dead behind and many weapons. In December of that year, President Lyndon Johnson awarded him the Medal of Honor in a White House ceremony.

When I was in Infantry Officers Candidate School at Fort Benning, Georgia, in 1966 and 1967, for six months we were mercilessly harassed physically, mentally, and emotionally as we tried to become second lieutenants in the U.S. Army. The only personal item we had that was not ready for inspection twenty-four hours per day was our locked footlockers. I kept a photograph of Roger taped inside the lid of my footlocker wearing his Medal of Honor neck ribbon, captain's bars, and green beret and looked at it and got inspired every time I opened that footlocker. Years later, in the early nineties, I met Roger and his lovely wife, Norma, as my wife, Shirley, and I sat with them at a banquet. I told him that story, and we became fast friends.

Then, about six years ago or so, Roger was asked to be the special guest of honor of a company of the Tenth Special Forces Group at the U.S. Army versus U.S. Air Force football game at the U.S. Air Force Academy in Colorado Springs. Norma fell ill shortly before the game, so Roger called me and asked me to go in his place as special guest of honor. I was so deeply humbled and appreciative of the first recipient of the Vietnam War to be awarded the coveted Medal of Honor asking me to stand in for him; words could not express my feelings. Roger is fighting another battle these days . . . Agent

Dedication

Orange–related Parkinson's disease, while I fight Agent Orange–related type 2 diabetes and heart disease.

Thank you for your heroism and inspiration and friendship, Roger. I love you, my friend.

This book is dedicated to these three heroes who have played such important roles in my life.

Don Bendell, 2016

ACKNOWLEDGMENTS

I must acknowledge my longtime close friend and former pastor Dr. Scott Middleton. Scottie Middleton, my character in this novel and its prequels *Blood Feather* and *The Indian Ring*, is named after him. A Texas boy originally, Scott has been a missionary in Scotland and created and heads Alba Ministries, which is still ongoing. He is the pastor of Craig Christian Church in Craig, Colorado, and is an adjunct professor of New Testament at Dallas Christian College. He has a doctor of ministry degree in pastoral theology from Highland Theological College. When my late wife passed away, Scott conducted her funeral, which she and I both requested when planning our funerals. He baptized me in the Arkansas River years ago, as well as two of my sons; and has been a confidant and very close friend to me for decades. He is my go-to man when I need a prayer to actually get through to God.

I want to also acknowledge another close friend and all that she represents. The summer before I started writing this, in June 2014, I was the official escort of a woman who became a very close friend. Anita LaCava Swift and I attended the Special Forces Association National Convention in Columbia, South Carolina, together, where she was a VIP guest and a featured speaker. Anita is the oldest grandchild of John Wayne and is the president of the John Wayne Cancer Institute Auxiliary. Even though he has been dead for years, John Wayne was recently chosen by fans as the second most popular movie star in the world. He had a significant influence on me growing up, and I have so much respect for the John Wayne family for carrying on his important fight against cancer, which he succumbed to himself. Every day I wear five Montagnard brass bracelets on my right wrist for the indigenous tribal people I lived with and fought beside in South Vietnam in 1968 and 1969. I also wear a leather bracelet with a little steel engraved plate reading COURAGE on one side and JOHN WAYNE FOUNDATION on the other. It was a treasured gift from Anita. She is not only a beautiful lady and a classy friend, but is typical of the John Wayne family in carrying on his legacy, and I guarantee that the Duke looks down fondly from Heaven on them with a great deal of pride. He, too, is wearing in Heaven, I'm certain,

Acknowledgments

his own Montagnard bracelet, which he received in 1968 while making the film *The Green Berets* and wore the rest of his life.

Scott and Anita, I love you both, my friends.

Don Bendell

FOREWORD

Phantom Canyon is not a creation of this writer's imagination. I have ridden its length many times in cars and have ridden much of it on horseback. Sitting a saddle while riding alone in Phantom Canyon, listening to the mountain breezes whistling through tall trees and rocky crevices, seeing the shapes and shadows as the sun advances overhead, and especially riding it after dark, which I have done, one can see how people could get spooked and unnerved. One might liken the experience to trying to make love to a grizzly bear: Although it may be a unique and colorful experience, it is nonetheless a tad unsettling.

Phantom Canyon wagon road was a twenty-five-mile-long real wagon and horse trail that became the Florence and Cripple Creek Narrow Gauge Railway in the 1890s, and which still exists today as a winding, scenic hard-packed road available for cars without trailers to travel between the old mining towns of Victor and Cripple Creek, on the western slope of Pikes Peak, and Florence, which, at 5,000 feet elevation, is 4,500 feet lower. Very popular tourist attractions along the way are the ghost towns of Wilbur, Adelaide, and Glenbrook, which were all swept away in flash floods. The scenic road has two large hand-dug tunnels and many twists and turns, with rising mountain cliffs and steep, high drop-offs. The route has a great deal of wildlife, which in the nineteenth century also included grizzly bears and wolves. It has always been rumored to harbor ghosts of executed fugitives from Old Max Penitentiary in nearby Cañon City as well as American Indian braves and other travelers who perished. Enjoy your adventure in Phantom Canyon.

1
THE TEAMSTER

Dub Tabor was a popular teamster, mainly operating out of Bent's Fort, far to the east of Pueblo on the Santa Fe Trail. Dub was given that moniker as a child, which made him eternally grateful, as his real name was Durwood, a label he dreaded. Dub had been a very energetic and precocious lad. He grew up the son of a farmer near Wichita, Kansas. Young Dub was always running, and his pa joked with his ma that he felt Dub might have actually not been his son but the offspring of a whitetail deer.

When he was a teenager, he watched teamsters with fascination and liked how they walked along the left side of their horses, mules, or oxen. It was a practice that decades later would prompt the positioning of the steering wheel, pedals, and instruments in automobiles. While still a teen, he got his first freight wagon and started hauling goods for various clients. Working his way to Bent's Fort on the Santa Fe Trail many miles out on the prairie from Pueblo, Colorado. Now in his late twenties, he had teams of horses, oxen, and mules and several wagons. He hired a handful of part-time teamsters, who he trained himself.

On this day, he was hauling supplies back from Cripple Creek, on the western slope of Pikes Peak, and was taking the scenic, but dangerous, Phantom Canyon road. Just after the sun set and the greens and browns of cliffs and trees started melting into each other, Dub walked along the wagon on the left side of the four bay horses, heads down, pulling the heavy load. They rounded another bend in the road, and he heard a noise off to his right. By the time he rounded two more bends, it was dark and pitch-black in the trees, excepting the sharp daggers of moonlight stabbing their way between branches and leaves. The moon glowing on the towering cliffs gave the whole scene an eerie look, and Dub felt a shiver run down his spine.

He stopped the horses with a gentle but firm "Whoa!" and turned to relieve himself right there on the road. His shoulders shivered as he did so, and he laughed at himself for being jumpy. However, he had the creepy feeling that someone or something was staring at him, and he heard sticks breaking in the trees behind him.

He suddenly had to go some more. Then, he turned and looked into the trees and saw a shadowy black form that stood maybe eight to ten feet tall.

Scared to death, he drew his old Schofield revolver and yelled, "Who's there?"

He saw the shadow farther down the trail, and it was moving fast through the trees. The size was enormous—wider than a grizzly bear, and much taller. His knees literally started shaking, and he fired a snapshot with the gun, knowing it was already out of range. The shot spooked the horses, and they bolted down the wagon road, merchandise in the back making louder noises banging in the wagon, which panicked them even more. His right hand was wrapped with one of the reins, which snapped around it like a bullwhip. Eyes bulging in panic, like his team of Morgans, Dub was dragged, with his right hand and arm being jerked up over his head. They rounded the next bend, and there was a cliff with a three-hundred-foot drop into a rocky canyon.

Seeing his life flash before his eyes, Dub was dragged toward the precipice, the horses now at full gallop, and he screamed as the first pair of hapless steeds ran right off the cliff, with the other two following, and pushing as well. His hand came free and his heart pounded wildly as Dub lay there watching all four horses and his wagon propel into blackness, only to hear them all crashing on the rocks seconds later, three hundred feet below.

He lay there at the edge of the darkened cliff, sides

heaving, heart pounding in his ears, and he thought the veins in the side of his neck might explode through the skin. His knees were shaking so badly, he couldn't stand, and now his stomach erupted as he vomited right over the edge of the cliff. His stomach hurt, and Dub stood on rubbery knees, having to relieve his bladder again.

Tears filled his eyes, and he got up, pacing back and forth near the cliff edge. The creature, the shadow, totally unnerved him. He had never been so frightened in his life.

No wonder they call this Phantom Canyon! he thought.

On shaky legs, he stumbled forward through the darkness, his eyes darting all around. He kept looking off to his right, trying to see that giant form again and praying he would not. Dub walked rapidly, dreading what he might see as he went around each bend and praying someone would venture along, but knowing they would not. This was not a busy road by any stretch.

Dub kept one leg stepping in front of another in what could only be described as a fast walk. All his senses were on alert, and tears stung his eyes as he moved. The tears were partially because of the sadness over losing his best wagon and team of horses, but also because of the wind whipping into his face as he walked rapidly southward, straining his eyes to identify every shadow, every shape.

Dub rounded a bend into total shadow and just listened. His heart pounded so hard it was all he could hear. Then he noticed he was breathing as if he had just run a race up the side of Pikes Peak. Fear gripped him like the claws of a cougar sinking into the flesh of a panicked prey. Then, in the moonlight, he saw the shadow back behind him, moving along the cliff. This was a smaller shadow, yet still very large. It was not the humongous beast he had seen, but something closer to the ground, yet silent.

Dub turned, half running, half fast-walking down Phantom Canyon wagon road. With every bend he went around, there were new goblins and new ghosts to haunt him.

The large tom mountain lion following Dub was indeed trailing him at a distance, but that was not unusual. This lion, like all his cousins and ancestors, quite often did trail people and animals down mountain roads and paths, especially after dark. It was just a natural predatory instinct, but like most big cats, this one would never attack a human unless it was cornered, though if the prey ran it might set off an attack. It did its best to stay out of sight of the occasional humans it saw or smelled. He also had winded not only the human, but his horses, and the large creature that passed by in the trees.

The human creature was walking rapidly down the road, but not moving fast enough to trigger the predatory attack response.

Dub was shivering, looking all around, his eyes

searching every shadow until they watered some more. He heard a loud snap of a branch down the road below him, and he stared into the blackness. His heart now pounded so hard, he really felt it would explode in his chest. The smaller figure behind him was large, but nothing like the one that had spooked his horses and him. It had been humongous. Dub did not know what to do, so he just moved quickly onward. The teamster did not want to run, as he might run right into the giant creature. He did not know that the decision actually prevented an attack by the cougar, as moving at a run surely would have triggered a charge.

His fast-walking continued for an hour, and at some point the mountain lion gave up the curious pursuit and returned to the smell of the dead horses that had gone over a cliff. Contrary to many beliefs, cougars did not really care much for the taste of beef, but they loved horseflesh. Ninety-eight percent of mountain lions' diet was deer, which they killed. They did not eat carrion, but the horses had just died, so the big cat would feed on them for several days, until the meat got a little tainted. The finicky cat would then abandon the meal and leave it for bears, coyotes, and other predators. Besides deer, cougars loved to eat skunks and porcupines, which they would reach under and flip on their backs, then biting their stomachs. However, these little critters only constituted two percent of a big cat's diet. Horses, especially newborn foals, were loved by pumas but hard to catch and kill. These horses that had just died would be a nice treat for the big tom for a few days. Unfortunately, Dub did not know that the cat was now long gone, and the fear of it would plague him, as well as that of the monster he was seemingly chasing down the long, winding canyon.

At every turn now, Dub wondered if the hideous creature was on one of the steep, shadowy cliffs often towering above the trail. He pictured a gargantuan monster ready to pounce on him and devour him. He had to stop, though. He had gone many miles much faster than he was used to traveling. His legs now felt like each step was calf-deep in quicksand, and he was sucking air, although he had been steadily dropping in elevation.

Rounding one bend, Dub spotted a large rocky overhang with a natural cavern going back into the mountain maybe forty feet in depth. He felt he could make a fire here and get some rest. A creek ran the length of the canyon, so water had not been a concern. He also wisely had carried a small emergency parfleche on his side with hardtack, jerked elk meat, matches, and bullets for his pistol. He soon had a small fire going in the back of the natural cavern, and despite his extreme fear, exhaustion took over, and he fell into a deep sleep.

At some point, Dub started having a nightmare, and in it a giant apelike creature was standing over him while he lay on the ground. It picked a large log out of the fire and let it cast light down on Dub, who was so frightened he could not get his legs to move. The shoulders were twice as muscular as a grizzly's and twice as wide, and the chest was more massive, too. The creature was standing and walked on two legs like a human and bared long fangs like a grizzly.

Dub wanted to scream but he could not get anything out of his mouth. Then the light from the burning log really bothered his eyes and the heat was getting unbearable. The creature started to make noises that sounded strangely like one of Dub's wagons, and it came even closer to his face. He gave a loud whimper and sat bolt upright, the bright morning sun shining directly into his face. His sides heaved in and out, and he looked all around. Dub pulled his old pocket watch out and saw that it was well past nine in the morning. He had not slept this long since the day after his wife had passed away from consumption.

It was then that Dub noticed the man. He sat in a small wagon, a two-wheeled wagon, loaded with some kind of goods, and the man was staring at Dub. The worn-out teamster jumped to his feet, wondering what was happening to him now. The man smiled and doffed his hat. Dub nodded, shivered, and turned to relieve his bladder. The man said that he had come out of Florence and was carrying supplies up to a mining claim he had filed miles up the road.

Bringing a coffeepot and some food over to the cavern, he gave his horse a rest and made breakfast for the two of them while Dub explained his tale. It was very obvious to the man that Dub was indeed frightened out of his wits. He did not know what to make of the monster

8

story, but he did not believe in spooks and haunts. Nonetheless, he caught himself looking all around at the surrounding cliffs and trees while they spoke.

The cougar was long gone and had fed on the horses earlier, but now was sleeping on a ledge above them. Mountain lions would make a kill, almost always a deer, by attacking from a short run or jumping from above, and would grab the prey on both sides of the body with their long, curved, retractable claws and then would bite the back of the spine in order to break the neck. After making the kill, a lion would feed on the intestines first, then the leg meat. After a first feeding, it would select a perch, as this one had, above the kill site and keep watch over it while it napped.

This particular tom would soon leave the horses, because a silvertip grizzly four miles away was now standing on its hind legs, nose testing the wind. Grizzlies' sense of smell, like that of all bears, was incredible. This big boar grizzly instinctively catalogued the smells entering his nostrils. He smelled some cedar trees, water from the creek, various human scents still coming off the road, and the smell of the crashed wagons, but beyond all, he smelled the spilled blood and meat of the horses. He would trot, nose working feverishly, downhill to the source of the smell. When he arrived, the cougar would begrudgingly slink away to search for more prey elsewhere. The grizzly would remain there and would not be a threat to Dub.

The man in the wagon offered to take Dub to Cañon City to the sheriff's department, an offer that the teamster gladly accepted. He just wanted to get home, and he could not wait to tell his story again, but he wondered if the sheriff would think he was drunk. They doused the fire, buried it, and loaded up. Dub was fast asleep within one minute, sitting up on the buckboard.

They had not gone a mile when a large mule deer buck bolted from some scrub oak along the road, and Dub, in shock, sat up and drew his pistol, firing at the shaking, small trees. The horses pulling the wagon bolted, eyes wide open in panic. The driver, Jerome Taylor, who had been dozing almost, was completely relaxed and was flung from his wagon seat, landing on his back, and his head hit a rock. He was knocked out cold. The wagon traces fell down between the horses, and Dub holstered his gun, his heart still pounding wildly as he stood on the wagon seat peering down for the flying reins. The horses, in full-panic flight mode, ran into the trees alongside the road now.

Panicked himself, Dub started yelling, "Whoa, boys! Whoa!"

It was almost dark when Jerome sat up, shaking his head and looking around. He was totally confused and disoriented. He stood on rubbery knees and walked over to a rivulet of water running down the roadside cliff. He cupped his hands, splashing water all over his face. Jerome did not know what had happened, but he did remember meeting this Dub hombre who'd scared him half to death with tales of a ten-foot-tall, hairy monster.

Thinking of that, he started moving ahead as quickly as he could on wobbly legs. His head ached horribly, but he had to head toward Cañon City. Jerome was very nervous, almost as bad as Dub had been. He finally came to a spot along the wide trail where he knew there was an overhang right below the rock outcropping he saw. He had weathered there five years earlier during a major spring thunderstorm. He would stay there, build a fire, and hope to be safe until daylight.

Jerome found the small cave and grabbed some squaw wood to start a fire. He soon had one going, and he then ventured out to break off some branches to make himself a bed. An hour later, he was fast asleep and slumbered fitfully.

In the morning, at full light, Jerome started walking . . . fast. He could not get to town soon enough. He saw the tracks of his stampeding horses and then figured he must have been thrown from his wagon. Following them around one of the many turns in the road, he gasped.

He clearly saw the tracks of his wagon and horses going into the trees, and there before him about eight feet up off the ground, he saw the limp figure of Dub Tabor, neck broken and wedged in the *V* of an extended, large cottonwood limb. The tracks told the story, and he hung his head down as he walked past the body. He could tell the man was wedged firmly into the tight *V* of the limb, and there was no way he could retrieve the body.

Two hours of walking brought him to the team and wagon. The horses, still in their harness, were grazing on tall green roadside grasses, and a small stream ran down the side of the ridgeline nearby. Jerome thought about going back with the wagon to cut the branch down and take the body back with him, but he thought better of it. The frightened man pictured every sort of monster imaginable, and he wondered if the phantom was watching him now. His mind raced as he tried to figure out what had happened. He clearly remembered his talk with Dub about the large, hairy, black creature he had seen that ran his team over the cliff, and about the creature stalking him. He remembered it was at least eight feet tall and wider than a pair of oxen.

It was all he could do to keep his panic in check and not run his horses to death all the way to the mouth of Phantom Canyon. Finally egressing the twisting, turning canyon, he went uphill for a mile or so and emerged at the beginning of the prairie stretching to the east. To his right was Cañon City, now only a few miles distant. In two hours, he pulled up in front of the Fremont County sheriff's office and tied his team at the hitching rail and watering trough out front. He had quite a tale to tell and knew many deputies and others would be going back to Phantom Canyon to investigate and retrieve the body. He wondered if they would want him to lead them back to where the body of Dub was hanging from the tree. That was the last thing he ever wanted to do. Jerome did not want to go to Phantom Canyon again. He now knew the legend about the phantom was not a tale. It was something to be feared, and he wondered if there was anybody, anywhere who could find and conquer the monster.

2

CHICAGO

Men tried to envision the shapely body and long, muscular legs under the classy gold lamé dress, while women watching the duo walking down the well-lit Chicago street marveled at the man at her side. He was much taller than other men, with a similar waistline to most, yet he had a chest and shoulders much larger than just about any man. The suit he wore strained to contain the bulging muscles all over his body. Properly tailored, it hid the specially designed Colt .45 Peacemaker with a tiny lawman's badge on either side of the ivory handle, an inheritance from his stern but fatherly stepdad. The back of his suit jacket also hid the large fringed and porcupine quill–decorated sheath of the razor-sharp, antler-handled Bowie-size knife, an inheritance from

his biological father, a Lakota warrior named Claw
Marks who left this man's white mother to a life that
would be productive and less complicated without a "red
savage" in her world.

The pair were leisurely walking and talking after
having dinner on Randolph Street, the site of numerous
restaurants in Chicago. As they passed under a gas
streetlamp, he looked over and stared into her deep
brown, smiling eyes. She did the same to him, and it
seemed as if they had aimed bows of passion at each
other loaded with arrows of desire. They stopped and
faced each other, and each of their lips slowly moved
toward the other's. The arrows had been released and
were flying true. Their lips came together.

"Well, lookee here, boys. One a them blanket niggers
come off the reservation and thinks he is gonna git hisself a white woman," came a voice from behind them.

They both pulled apart, and the man, Joshua Strongheart, pushed her protectively behind him. He faced the
gang of five who had come up behind him. All of them
were obviously drunk. They also were all angry railroad
workers, taking part in the nationwide railroad strike
that had begun a month earlier in Baltimore and quickly
spread across the country. These ruffians were angry at
the management of several railroad lines, but were now
focusing their anger on Strongheart, the half-breed pre-
mier Pinkerton agent.

The beauty, Brenna Alexander, tried to step around

Joshua to confront the men, too, but Strongheart's sinewy arm pushed her back out of harm's way.

He turned and softly commanded, "Brenna, go sit on that bench. I'll just be a minute."

Seeing the command presence he had when he spoke, she immediately went to the nearby street-side bench and sat obediently. This man was in charge right now in the face of danger, and she was glad. She had seen him in action before, when her Indiana mansion was burned to the ground while she and Joshua barely escaped. Like her father before her, Brenna abhorred racism and was active in the Underground Railroad, smuggling slaves and oppressed sharecroppers from the South to more freedom and paying jobs in the North and Midwest.

The worker who had made the initial comment was a big, beefy man with wide shoulders, a barrel chest, and massive arms from years of laying railroad ties and driving in spikes.

The man guffawed and started to make a comment, but Joshua's hand came up quickly, palm toward the man's face. Joshua's mind was working rapidly. He was facing five large, muscular men, and he preferred defusing this situation and getting back to the lovely Brenna. He had no desire to fight, especially with the odds so much against him. He knew a fight was inevitable unless he could stop the five in their tracks.

Joshua said, "Before you say anything else here, let's

save a lot of time. It is obvious to me that you are spoiling for a fight, and I have become your target. So, will I only have to fight you, or all five of you?"

The big man looked at the other four and started chuckling.

"What do you think, blanket nigger?" he replied with a deep, bellowing laugh.

Strongheart said, "Well, sir, that sure makes it acceptable for me to use any tools I need to get this job done. So, first, let me show you something."

He walked over to one of the behemoths, who was holding a large mug half-filled with frothy beer.

He gently took him by the forearm, smiling, and said, "Please, sir. Just help me out a second."

The man, in his drunken stupor, followed Strongheart's direction as he moved him so a vacant lot was behind him.

Joshua backed off about twenty feet and said, "Now, sir, please hold the mug of beer out to your side."

Not knowing how to respond, the man did just that.

Joshua said, "Thank you. Now, without anybody counting, or saying anything, simply let go of the glass anytime you want."

The man did so, and before the mug of beer fell even one foot, it exploded with the blast of a Colt .45. All looked, and that quickly, Joshua had reacted, drawn his pistol, and fired from the hip. Brenna had never seen anybody draw a gun so fast in her life, and nor had any of the striking railroad workers.

One said, "Did you see that?"

The man next to him said, "No. I ain't never seen anybody draw so fast, or accurate."

Strongheart grinned sadistically and said, "All right, gentlemen. There are five of you, and I have five bullets left in my shooter, plus six more in my belly gun. I'm ready to fight."

They looked at each other and back at him and put their hands up in a pleading manner.

The bully said, "Mister, I am very sorry. I did not mean no disrespect."

Strongheart said, "Well, each of you owes my young lady here an apology, as you disrespected her."

All five of them started bowing and apologizing to her, removing their hats. They walked backward, increasing their speed as they moved down the street.

Brenna walked up to him, smiling, and wrapped her arms around his neck, kissing him passionately.

She stepped back, looking up into his eyes, and said, "Joshua Strongheart, you are the most amazing man I have ever known. I feel so safe with you. You can handle any problem that would ever come up."

He said, "No, it is just a lot harder not to fight than it is to fight, but not fighting is usually the right thing to do."

She wrapped her hands around his beefy arm, and they walked down the street.

He smiled at her as they walked along and said, "William Shakespeare wrote, 'I must be cruel, only to be kind.'"

She just shook her head and chuckled. She was falling deeply in love with her hero. He never ceased to amaze her.

Joshua Strongheart was a Pinkerton agent, the stepson of a quiet, unassuming Montana lawman, and the love child of a mighty Lakota warrior named Claw Marks and a beautiful and hardy fifteen-year-old orphan girl who settled in Montana and ended up marrying Marshal Dan Trooper. They were all gone now. Strongheart was taken often to the village of his late father to learn the Lakota ways. At home, Dan was a strict but loving father figure who taught him how to be a good man who could fight with guns or fists better than just about anyone. His mother, who was a self-made, successful merchant, ensured he got an education, including a penchant for quoting Shakespeare.

Strongheart was left with a nice inheritance from his mother, as her mercantile was very successful for years. He knew he had to find a job he would be totally passionate about, and he did find it. He was a Pinkerton agent and the apple of Allan Pinkerton's eye. This organization was the forerunner of the United States Secret Service and was the premiere private detective agency of the entire world.

The couple walked on to Brenna's house, and no sooner were they inside than there was a knock on the door. Hand on his pistol, Joshua stood by the door while Brenna answered it.

A man stood there in a brown suit, and he tipped his

hat to Brenna and said, "Agent Strongheart, they want you at headquarters right away. Sorry to interrupt, sir."

Strongheart said, "I'll saddle my horse and be there shortly. Thank you. Are you new?"

"Second day, sir."

One hour later, Joshua Strongheart walked into the lantern-lit office of Lucky Champ, his French-born supervisor and friend.

"Bonsoir, mon ami," Strongheart said. *"Comment allez-vous?"*

Lucky smiled. *"Je vais bien, merci, monsieur. Et vous?"*

"Bien, merci, boss. What's up?"

Lucky said, "We have trouble times two brewing in your home territory. The Fremont County sheriff has sent several telegraphs to us. It seems there is a place near Cañon City called Phantom Canyon? *N'est-ce pas?"*

Joshua said, "Yeah, I've ridden it. It runs up to the southern and western slopes of Pikes Peak. Narrow wagon road, lots of twists and turns, cliffs, and forest. If some of those prospectors poking around Pikes Peak hit gold or silver, I guarantee it will become a railroad right-of-way."

Little did Strongheart know how prophetic that statement was, as that would occur in less than a decade.

Lucky went on. "Apparently, the people down there are nervous, thinking there really is a phantom or something scary in Phantom Canyon. Somebody has been killed and there have been several incidents, and the sheriff would like your help in tracking whatever it is. Also, we have been hired because there is trouble brewing, with a possible railroad war beginning. You are going to investigate and try to avert it if you can."

"Well, so much for a few days off," Joshua said merrily. "I guess trouble never stops. I will take the train at daybreak."

3

THE PHANTOM NEVER SLEEPS

Wannge'e grew up in the Four Corners area, where Colorado, Utah, Arizona, and New Mexico came together. As many members of the Ute tribe did, he had blended into white society and had been working as a scout, leading white men out on hunting and fishing expeditions or taking them into the wilderness to search for areas they wanted to prospect. Although his Ute name meant "Red Fox," white men called him Juan Jay, or just Juan, as it was the closest name to his real name of Wannge'e. Also like many Utes, he spoke English well.

Wannge'e had heard the stories which were circulating all around southern Colorado now about the phantom of Phantom Canyon, the death, the fear, the crashed wagon and dead horses. He heard descriptions of a creature that moved fast and was as tall as a tall man holding another tall man on his shoulders. He heard that the creature was as wide in the shoulders as a small horse is long. Thinking of all the stories he heard, Wannge'e was certain that Phantom Canyon had become the home of at least one *Pahi-zoho*, also called *Si-Te-Cah*. He had met a Nez Perce at Bent's Fort one day, and they got into a discussion about the *Pahi-zoho*. The Nez Perce, who was from the Oregon area, told him that some white men who had seen the *Pahi-zoho* called it a Bigfoot, because its tracks were so large. He said in their country many large ones had been seen, as well as females still taller than any man, and young ones, too. The shoulders on the male were as "wide as a man lying on his side is long," and some were as "tall as two men, one standing on the other."

He was frightened, yet fascinated.

The sound of many crickets deep in Phantom Canyon was haunting, and the trees and overhanging cliffs were stingy about letting shards and slivers of moonlight shine through them. The crickets stopped suddenly. Wannge'e awakened and sat straight up, looking all about him. He blinked his eyes at the shadows, and suddenly movement to his left front caught his eyes. He felt a shiver run up and down his spine; he had to quickly stand up and relieve his bladder. He shivered again while he did so.

He could hear his heart pounding in his ears as he

caught movement again, in the trees. He now felt his heart thumping in his chest, and he shook his head. It felt like it was full of lard, and he could not think clearly. His knees were shaking so hard, he thought whatever it was could see them shake.

More movement, and this time it was from the shadows in the trees and undergrowth, and it seemed to be getting closer, looming larger and larger and larger. It was the shape of a man, now behind some branches and trunks, but it must have been ten feet tall. It had long hair all over its body, and its muscles, even in the shadows, were clearly enormous compared to those of any man Wannge'e had ever seen. Thrice the size of the strongest man Juan Jay had witnessed in his life. Paralyzed by fear, he could not move.

The beast moved closer and now was standing clearly visible in the moonlight less than twenty feet away. Wannge'e wanted to scream, but his vocal cords would not work.

He had been this close to a massive boar silvertip grizzly one time, but this monster looked twice as powerful as the mighty bear. It was built like a man, but its arms were much longer, seeming to hang almost down to its knees. What was most eerie, though, were the eyes. With a full moon brightly illuminating the creature, the eyes looked humanlike, but they were bright red. This was the same look he had seen in the eyes of owls before when he cast a torchlight on them. That made the whole scene even more scary. It had not walked like a bear balancing on its hind legs either, but more effortlessly, like an athlete, a giant man. Wannge'e had a friend who had traveled back East with some white men and had seen monkeys and apes and described them in full detail. This looked like a giant version of what his friend had described, but walking and moving upright like a human.

Wannge'e felt if this *Pahi-zoho* took one more step forward, he might faint, he was so frightened. He had never been so scared in all his life. He could tell the creature could move rapidly, and he felt if it grabbed him it was strong enough to literally rip his arms or legs off. He wondered if this thing considered him prey to be killed and eaten.

It stepped forward, and Wannge'e yelled as he turned to run and his legs got tangled up, tripping him. He hit the ground hard, then pushed himself up with his hands as his eyes came open. He looked around and saw only the glowing embers in his campfire. His feet were tangled up in his blanket, and his horse was calmly grazing in the grass nearby. His breaths came out in heaving sobs almost.

He had been dreaming. It was a nightmare—the worst he had ever experienced—but it all seemed so real. He was panting like a dog now, and he put some sticks on the fire, instinctively feeling the additional light and warmth would make him safer. Wannge'e had been "over the mountain and down the river" a time or two, and nothing had ever frightened him like this. He put his pot of coffee on the fire and waited for it to heat up. He knew he would be awake a long time now.

An hour passed, and the adrenaline coursing through Wannge'e's body was starting to wear down. His eyelids became heavy, and he blinked continuously, staring into the shadows, which frequently seemed to be moving. His eyes scanned across an open area in the trees and looked up the road to his right, toward the distant, unseen Pikes Peak. Then he swept his gaze back, and suddenly in the open space, there was a creature, and now Wannge'e was not asleep. This was not a dream. Something very wide, very tall, and very black moved from the opening, and made noise doing so. It was much wider than a bear would be, and much taller, even than a grizzly bear.

Wannge'e left his coffeepot, his pack, his water bag, and everything but his rifle, and leapt up onto his horse's back, leaving his saddle behind as well. He grabbed the mane of the big bay and kicked him hard in both ribs, heading back south and hoping he could make Cañon City alive. He bent low over the horse's neck and the bay sensed danger was behind them as he lit out as if his tail were set ablaze. As the trail fell behind him, Wannge'e relaxed his senses a little bit more and, after a mile, slowed to a trot.

He kept on at a trot, periodically slowing to a walk, lest he kill his horse. Then, when the horse seemed to catch his breath, he would kick him back into a trot. More than an hour passed before he finally let the horse stop and rest along the trail. Wannge'e dared to dismount, and he put his ear to the ground, listening intently. Coincidentally, three mule deer who had let him pass by minutes earlier were now spooked by another noise farther up the road, and they bounded off in their hopping style, reminiscent of giant four-legged kangaroos. Juan Jay heard the drumming sound in the ground, and his eyes opened as wide as silver dollars. He made a mad dash for his horse and leapt onto his back, sending him south again in a panicked canter. The horse was well-lathered before he slowed the mustang gelding down again.

The frightened Ute was miles down the canyon and it was well after daybreak before he dismounted again and led his horse at a fast walk. His eyes scoured the trail and, off to his right, within a half mile, he spotted something that made him freeze in his tracks. He looked down, and there, hardened in the mud, were the footprints, heading north, of a barefooted man. They had been made when the ground was wet from rain two days earlier, but what sent shivers up and down his spine was the size of the tracks. They clearly looked humanlike, but were thirty percent wider than any human footprint and were seventeen or eighteen inches in length. They were also very, very deep into the dried mud. Staring at the tracks, which he assumed were from the creature who had confronted him, Wannge'e shivered and felt a chill run up and down his spine. He had to relieve his bladder again and shivered the same way twice more while doing so.

This *Pahi-zoho* was not just a menacing, frightening creature; it was also enormous compared to stories he had heard about other sightings and tracks. The Ute wondered how close to death he had been.

Two skeptical deputies from the Fremont County sheriff's office rode out of Cañon City the next morning to head up Phantom Canyon to where the very frightened Indian had seen the tracks. They both were no longer skeptical when they did see the tracks. They both had to relieve their bladders and both also shivered while doing so. One was wise enough to hang a red kerchief from an overhanging branch to mark the unnerving tracks. They returned at a fast trot most of the way to make their report to the sheriff. They both had gone after escaped prisoners from Old Max. Both had been on the search for a large killer grizzly and had been in on the capture of several dangerous outlaws, but no experience compared with this one. The two men were frightened and wondered how this monster could be killed. They wondered if it could be, and who could do it.

4

PROTECT YOUR HOME

Joshua Strongheart had been gone from southern Colorado for a couple weeks and was very glad to be home. His late fiancée, Annabelle Ebert, had left him her home and her Cañon City restaurant. Joshua never slept in the home after her death. He traded it for a small spread along the Arkansas River toward Florence, and he gave the restaurant to Belle's niece, who came in from Missouri to operate it. He also never went there to eat again.

Wannge'e wanted to scream, but no words would come out of his mouth. The *Pahi-zoho* had a hold of his upper arm and was shaking him. His head was gigantic and shaped like an upside-down funnel. His eyes were flaming, and his teeth had fangs like the largest grizzly. Wannge'e was once again paralyzed with fear.

The *Pahi-zoho* said, "Wannge'e! Wannge'e!" and he sat bolt upright, blinking his eyes against the bright sunlight streaking in through the window of the sheriff's office. He looked straight up into the grinning face of the handsome Joshua Strongheart, his hand on Wannge'e's upper arm. The confused Ute looked around and shook his head. Now he remembered the sheriff had let him sleep on a cot in the sheriff's office.

Strongheart said, "Hello, my red brother. I am Wanji Wambli of the Lakota nation, but my given name is Joshua Strongheart."

Wannge'e said, "I am of the Ute nation and am called Wannge'e, but you know that. I know of you—many stories of you. You are a Pinkerton and a mighty warrior with many, many scars."

"I have some scars," Joshua said, grinning. "How about getting up, and I will buy you a nice breakfast and lots of coffee. Then, we can smoke a cigar and talk."

"This is a good thing, Strongheart."

After breakfast, they went out behind the restaurant and walked to a large oak and sat down smoking cigars and watching the fast-moving Arkansas River flowing before them. Becoming animated, Wannge'e explained his misadventure in full detail.

Eyes opened wide, Wannge'e said, "This was a *Pahi-zoho*, Strongheart. I have not seen one before, but have heard their howls and have seen their tracks. I have met mighty warriors who have seen them."

Joshua listened and absorbed. He did not prejudge or make the Ute feel doubted. He wanted all the facts so he could unravel this mystery.

Wannge'e told Strongheart about the clear tracks now dried in hardened mud. The sheriff had already told Joshua his deputies had marked the spot. He would have to leave as soon as possible and not risk a storm washing out any more sign. Several days had passed already.

Joshua would leave before daybreak. In fact, he decided to leave then and ride the ten or so miles to the beginning of Phantom Canyon and camp there so he could be on the road at daybreak looking for sign.

Eagle seemed to understand they were on another great adventure as Joshua rode west out of town. The big black-and-white pinto tossed his mane from side to side and flipped his tail over his rump. Then, he went into one of his trotting gaits, which Joshua Strongheart referred to as his "floating gait." The horse would start trotting, and, getting excited, trot stiff-legged at a very fast pace, almost like he was floating above the ground. As he rode out of Cañon City, Strongheart had mountains to his west, north, and south and he went slightly uphill along the piñon- and scrub oak–covered hills that started the foothills of Pikes Peak and Cheyenne Mountain far to his north. Joshua looked at the varying rock formations and the prairie that was starting to slowly open up in front of him to the east. Leaving the greenery of the treetops behind him along the Arkansas River, he went up a long hill, and at the crest of that ridge, he came to a wagon road running to his right a few miles distant to Florence, and to his left, or north, it headed toward a canyon mouth that looked like it was innocent enough. However, Joshua knew this was the mouth of Phantom Canyon. He only needed to ride a mile and a half and the trail would start dropping down into the mouth of the rock- and tree-lined canyon.

A mile inside the rugged, narrow canyon, Strongheart made camp for the night. A stream ran alongside the narrow road off to his left, and heavy trees surrounded him, with large cliffs jutting up through them. There was plenty of graze for Eagle and clear water running in the creek. He did not anticipate any problems this night, as he was barely into the canyon.

Joshua had heard of these creatures, but in the Lakota language, the *Pahi-zoho* was referred to as *Iktomi*, which translates to "the Trickster." It was the animal that some whites had been calling a Bigfoot.

Strongheart, in the short period he had been back, could tell there was a panic going on about the phantom in Phantom Canyon, even among the local sheriff's deputies and the guards at Old Max. Many believed it was indeed a Bigfoot-type creature, and Strongheart knew and believed that they existed. However, he was certain there were very few around here. Most were in the Northwest, where there were plenty of deer, plenty

of rain, lots of streams and rivers, and many large, for-
ested areas with big trees. He had spoken to too many
Nez Perce who'd had run-ins with such creatures and had
a lot of credibility with Joshua as experienced warriors
who knew what they were doing.

He felt that the semiarid parts, and even the mountain-
ous parts, of southern Colorado would not be an environ-
ment suitable for such creatures. He had been out alone
often in the mountains and had not seen tracks or sign of
one. He also had occasionally heard trees being struck,
but always chalked that up to a branch falling or a rock
rolling off a cliff and hitting a tree trunk. A few times,
he did have branches, or even rocks, land near him on the
ground. He had heard of such activities by the *Iktomi*, but
he chalked his experiences up to natural phenomena.
Colorado was a land of more rocks than there were grains
of sand in the Sahara desert. It seemed only reasonable
to him that sometimes rocks would fall or roll for the
slightest reason. Tree branches often fall in the forest, as
do whole trees, sometimes from the lightest breeze.

One time, he was talking to his friend from Cotopaxi,
old Zachariah Banta, and Zach addressed the horse he
had given Joshua being half-Arabian and half-saddlebred.
Arabians were known to be very intelligent horses,
extremely stable and calm when well broke.

Zach made the statement, "Wal, Strongheart, I
reckon in this here country, we got rocks that sometimes
decide ta move. When they do move, ya want a horse
unner ya that don't."

Strongheart made camp for the night and slept soundly, knowing his "warrior's sense" would alert him if trouble started brewing or danger approached. Warriors have a sixth sense more highly developed than that of most people. It is a sense of knowing when danger is approaching. In trying to explain this to Lucky, Joshua asked if he ever got a chill-down-his-spine feeling when someone was looking at him from behind. Lucky responded that he had such an experience when a man he was investigating watched him at night looking into a house through a window behind him. Lucky whirled and saw the man just as he was pulling out a derringer to shoot at the Pinkerton. Strongheart explained that was the "warrior's sense of knowing," something that was very developed in men, and women, whose lives depended on always being alert. When hunting, especially with a bow, he explained that he never looked directly at an animal but right behind its tail for that very reason. Prey animals, such as deer and elk, can sometimes sense when they are being watched closely. He further explained that was why some hunters could not understand why they spooked game at the last second when they made no noise and the wind was not blowing.

Shortly before dawn he came out of a sound sleep, his Colt Peacemaker drawn and his eyes straining against the predawn darkness. He heard a light whinny from Eagle, who was grazing nearby, and he looked at Eagle's ears and eyes to see where he was focusing.

They centered on a small break in the trees, and Joshua saw several mule deer slowly walking between the shadows, headed downhill. Any large predator around probably would have alerted them, so Strongheart immediately went back to sleep.

He awakened right at dawn and cleaned up in the little creek, then made breakfast and thought about what he would do that day. He soon saddled up after two cups of coffee and some food and headed up the road toward Cripple Creek.

An hour later, the muscular Pinkerton agent spotted a red scarf tied to a branch on the left side of the road, and he dismounted, going forward slowly and retrieving the scarf. The deputies had wisely placed long branches as a border around the dried tracks in the mud to discourage deer and other grazing animals, or any simply passing through. Joshua, as he approached, could already see that they looked like very large barefoot human tracks with large spaces in between. The stride would fit with a human maybe nine or ten feet tall. A shiver ran down Strongheart's spine, but he shook that off, knowing it was a normal human reaction to such a sight. He was tracking now and was a warrior trained to track. Not quite as good as his friend Chris Colt, up near Westcliffe, but much better than most any man around, red or white.

He dropped his reins so Eagle would ground-rein automatically and not move until Strongheart raised the reins again. If he left the reins over the saddle horn, Eagle would follow him, but if they were dropped, he was trained not to move. This was easily accomplished by burying several logs with attached lead lines coming out of the ground. Joshua would stop the paint at each one, dismount, and subtly hook the lead line under the bridle. In that manner, Eagle would try to take a step and could not move. Horses are pattern animals and stick to preset patterns. When Strongheart did this a few times, it became ingrained in the big pinto's brain not to move if the reins were dropped.

Strongheart got down on his hands and knees and started to closely examine the tracks. No sooner had he started looking than he heard the clicking of three guns behind him. He turned slowly and saw three prospectors or miners who had just come around the bend in the road to his front. One was pointing a Henry rifle at him, while the other two were pointing pistols. All three were on foot.

"Wal, wal, wal," said the rifleman. "Lookee here, boys. We caught us a thievin' red blanket nigger. Where did ya put our horses, redskin?"

Strongheart said, "There has been a misunderstanding, gentlemen. I am a Pinkerton agent, not a thief."

The man just to the rifleman's left, Foster Shane, said "Naw, you ain't. Yer a blanket nigger, and thet makes you one a mah favorite targets. Jest shoot him, Blackie. We'll find the horses."

He laughed at his own comment.

Luke Blackwell, the rifleman, said, "Naw, we're gonna hang this ole redskin. The only good Injun is a dead Injun."

Strongheart bristled. He had heard that quote attributed to both General Philip Sheridan and seventh U.S. president Andrew Jackson; he doubted if either had said it. But, having just finally helped speed the demise of the notorious Indian Ring, Joshua knew that saying was the sentiment among many white men.

Tactically, he knew he was in trouble and needed an immediate plan. The man on the right who had not spoken, Dane Mathews, had dangerous eyes, and Strongheart noticed the holster was worn at the top from the man practicing quick draw a lot. The rifleman would be the next to go, as he could not move the rifle as quickly, and the one to his left, Foster Shane, would be third. Joshua had to disarm them for a minisecond anyway.

He said, "Listen, I am a Pinkerton agent and can show you all my badge and credentials."

Luke Blackwell, whose family owned a plantation along the Peedee in the Sandhills of North Carolina, said, "I don't care what lie you wanna yarn. We found yer moccasin tracks outside our mine last night, an dey was leadin' away our horses. Dane, git a rope."

The one to Blackwell's right started to take a step, and that was exactly what Joshua needed. The half-breed's hand whipped down to his Colt .45 Peacemaker, brought it out cocked, and fired. Flame stabbed from the barrel, and a big red spot on Dane's rib cage appeared as he folded like a suitcase. Strongheart's left hand fanned the hammer, and flame stabbed out again, and a bright red spot appeared in the middle of Luke's nose and the back of his head literally exploded. Strongheart's left hand fanned the hammer again, and that shot hit the left one, Foster, in the stomach a split second after he fired the bullet kicking up dirt between Strongheart's legs. The three bullets had been fired in less than a second, but the third did not hit the man squarely in the stomach, and Joshua fanned the hammer again and shot Foster again, dead center in the chest. He swayed and fell forward on his face, very dead.

Without thinking, Joshua started ejecting spent cartridges and thumbing new ones into the revolver as he walked forward, watching all three for any signs of life. Shane's legs were spasming slowly and involuntarily, but he was dead. All three were indeed dead.

Strongheart just shook his head thinking about what a shame it was that they had to die. He knew it was their choice, and they obviously were terrible racists, but they were men, and he did not want to kill anybody. They simply had given him no choice. He wondered, as he usually did after a gunfight, if he would not be happier running a ranch or a business. Then he smiled to himself, knowing better. Strongheart was a warrior, a man of the West. Adrenaline made him feel alive, and he was a protector.

Joshua knelt down by the body of Luke and went through his trousers and shirt pockets, looking for any signs of identification, and found a few dollars and nothing more. He set this aside to put in an envelope from his saddlebags; the collected money would probably help to pay the undertaker. The same was repeated, with the second search retrieving only small change. However, in the pocket of the third shooter, Dane, he found a small tintype of a beautiful young woman. With it was a short letter that read:

> *Dane, I love you so, my darling betrothed. Why did you forsake me, my love? Why won't you please forget this terrible quest for gold and return to me? I am heartbroken and miss you desperately. I don't need riches or treasures. I just need you.*

> *Love,*
> *Esmerelda*

When Joshua finished reading this, he noticed he had a tear rolling down each cheek, and he thought again of Belle, the woman he loved so much who had been brutalized and murdered by the seven-foot-tall behemoth We Wiyake, Blood Feather, whom he had in turn hunted down and killed. He had pretty much come to terms now with the guilt he felt over Belle's death, but he knew he would never forget her totally and would always grieve. However, he did give himself permission to love again and essentially keep on living.

Within an hour, a rider came by, and Strongheart sent him to fetch the sheriff's posse and the coroner, or whoever was coming to get the bodies. He would give a full report later, but for now, he prepared the bodies to be transported.

Then, he got back to his tracking in the immediate area where the footprints had dried in the mud. Strongheart remembered his friend Chris Colt had said to him that tracks always told a story, and you had to figure out what was going on in the person's mind or what instincts were going on in the animal's mind you were tracking. This could help you assemble a trail when tracks disappeared or were covered up for a distance.

Ben Shaffer was the current sheriff of Fremont County, Colorado, which also included what would become Custer County in just a couple more years. He was very curious about all these reports about the creature of Phantom Canyon, so he accompanied his deputies to the scene of the shooting, arriving at mid-afternoon. By that time, Joshua had solved the mystery of this set of tracks.

Joshua gave a report about the gunfight to the sheriff and his deputies and handed them the envelope with the contents of his attackers' pockets. Joshua had proven his word was iron, so he would not be questioned further about the incident. The sheriff also promised Strongheart he would write the young lady, whose address was on her note.

Strongheart said, "Follow me, Sheriff. I'll show you what I have come up with."

He took the sheriff to the tracks that had been discovered, and the lawman gave out a long, low whistle.

The sheriff said, "Those strides are way, way too long for any man, even one over seven foot tall. The man who left those footprints had to be nine or ten feet tall at least. Look at the size of those tracks. I could fit both my cowboy boots inside each barefoot track and still have room."

Strongheart grinned, saying, "What do you suppose it is?"

The sheriff said, "I guess that monster people keep talking about."

Joshua chuckled and said, "Sheriff, those tracks were made by a snowshoe hare running."

"What?" the sheriff replied, astonished.

Strongheart said, "I have seen them in melting snow before. These were tracks made by a leaping hare. When it hit the soft mud, its whole backside would come down on the ground, and he would leap off his hind legs, which would be a little forward of the rump. After snow starts melting, or in this case when the hare hit on wet mud or clay, it made the front of the track look like it had toes like a giant human that is barefoot. Look at the tracks more closely and you will find where the smaller front feet hit as well. Hitting in soft mud or in snow, then especially when the snow melts a little, a running snowshoe hare will make tracks that, from their fannies and all four feet hitting, look like a giant human barefoot track with strides six or seven feet long."

The sheriff literally got down on his hands and knees and studied the tracks and saw exactly what Strongheart suggested.

He stood, saying, "I'll be go to the dickens. You are absolutely right, Strongheart. But how did the horses or man get killed?"

Joshua said, "I didn't say anybody was wrong about the creature in Phantom Canyon. I was just showing you these tracks. I have only begun to search and I have eliminated one piece of evidence. That does not mean a giant creature does not exist like people are saying."

The sheriff said, "Well, you're right about all that, Strongheart. What is it that your father's folks call them?"

Joshua said the Lakota call them by two different names. "One is *Iktomi*, which means 'the Trickster.' The other name is *Chiye Tanka*, which means 'Big Elder Brother.' The Utes have another name, and so do all the other nations."

The lawman asked, "Do you believe they exist?"

Strongheart said, "Absolutely, but I am not certain they live in the Colorado area. More in the Northwest, I think, where there is much more rain, big trees, lots of deer—plus vegetation and lots of water. That seems to be important to these critters."

"What kind of critter do you figure they are?"

Joshua replied, "Very large, gigantic really, very smart apes, almost as smart as humans. From those I have spoken to, they speak to each other in a way. They signal each other by hitting trees with rocks and hitting rocks with rocks, with the number of hits giving a certain message. They have different howls and chatter, too. Two men I know who are Nez Perce in the Washington and Oregon area say they have seen them speaking to each other in a simple sign language and different crude speech patterns."

"You sound pretty sure about them?" the sheriff said.

"Yep," Joshua replied, "I am positive."

"Why so positive?"

Strongheart said, "In our tribe we have no word for lying or untruth. It is something that would get you banished for life. Many tribes and nations are that way. I have had several red brothers swear to me stories about seeing them. They simply would not lie or be mistaken."

Joshua broke a twig off a tree and picked something out of his teeth, then added, "I will keep heading north, looking for sign, and camping out along the way. If it is aggressive, it will come to me."

The sheriff said, "Well, after killing a seven-foot mad killer and a giant grizzly, let alone a gang of gunmen, if anybody could take on a ten-foot-tall monster that kills horses and men, it would be you, Strongheart. Be careful."

Joshua stuck out his hand and then whistled. Eagle trotted up to him, and he grabbed the saddle horn with his left hand and easily swung up into the saddle. He winked at the sheriff and rode north. One of the deputies waved at him and Joshua smiled back, nodding his head.

So many times he had been called "half-breed,"

"blanket nigger," "red nigger," and other derisive terms by men who could not pronounce or spell half the words in Joshua's vocabulary. However, the respect he had been shown here by folks from his town—even the simple act of a deputy waving as he left—it made up for a lot.

5

THE MONSTER

The tall Pinkerton agent rode northward at a slow walk, his eyes methodically sweeping back and forth in thirty-foot arcs directly in his path. Every minute or so, he would glance up into the trees and the cliffs that rose above him, his eyes scanning them for any trace of movement. Occasionally, he would look behind him and memorize his backtrail and watch for danger. In the mountains especially, trails do not always look the same going back on them as they do going forward, so Joshua would check to identify landmarks and see the view for when he made the return trip. At ten-minute intervals, he would simply stop and listen, and Eagle would always sense this and listen, too.

Strongheart slowly rode northward, carefully looking

for sign along both sides of the wagon trail. He would make camp under an overhang well before dark so that he would be able to walk all around and check where danger might come from. Based on the reports he had heard from the sheriff and statements he had read, he was certain that the creature would hunt him, if there was a creature. He had already proven that one piece of the puzzle had a very simple natural explanation. Maybe he would discover that the rest of the story could be easily explained. He knew that many people in the area were spooked, but he also knew that people, most people, seem to almost want a boogeyman in their lives. Maybe it made folks feel more alive. Joshua did not know if this creature was real or not, but he would find out soon. Eagle would alert him if something approached, and Joshua knew that no animal of any size would spook Eagle over a cliff.

Joshua kept this up for hours and by late afternoon found himself at a much-used overhang with several old campfires in it. He saw why the others stopped here, with the shelter of the overhang and towering cliff above as well as the stream near the road and good graze. Unsaddling Eagle, he let him graze along the roadside wearing a halter and long lead line. He found where the wagon and horses had gone over and scoured that area, on hands and knees at times. Then he returned to his campsite and started preparing it. He wanted a good rest, because he felt whatever it was might stalk or approach him during the night, and he wanted to be ready. Joshua found the largest campfire and dug it out better and placed more rocks around the rim. He built a fire with available wood and made a bed of pine boughs. Strongheart made his dinner and a pot of coffee. It was still light out, but he wanted to get some rest while he could. The next day, he would find the remains of the horses that had gone off the cliff and would check them to see what predators had fed on them. He would look for older tracks, as well as bite and claw marks and the type of feeding done on the horse carcasses.

For now, however, he would see if he got stalked at night. He would have a comfortable bed and try to get some good sleep early, because he felt he might not rest much that night. Joshua had been through too much and been around too long now to worry about what might happen. He knew that most people would actually terrify themselves with the unknown. He did have an unsettled feeling simply because of the gossip and the fact that there were dead people. However, Joshua had been up against some incredibly dangerous, threatening adversaries before, and he felt confident he could handle whatever challenged him.

Satisfied he had looked carefully at every possible avenue of enemy or predator approach, Joshua lay down before it was fully dark out and carefully set his holster close by, so he could reach over and draw his gun or knife quickly and easily. He almost immediately fell asleep.

It was not that long after darkness fell that Joshua's

eyes came open. He froze, and he immediately took mental inventory of his surroundings. He looked at his campfire, which still had flames, so he knew he had not been asleep that long. His eyes searched the darkness, and then he caught sight of Eagle, who had stopped grazing. His head was up, ears forward, and his nose was testing the wind, facing south on the edge of the wagon road. Something was beyond Eagle in the darkness. Something was coming.

Joshua's right hand slowly went forward and grabbed the handle of his Peacemaker.

The predator could now see the glow of Joshua's campfire on the roof of the cliff overhang up ahead. Eagle would have been in view but was now gone. The predator moved forward slowly, eyes searching carefully, methodically for the big black-and-white horse he had already seen. This was the predator causing so much panic. This beast was what was responsible for the deaths of four horses and a man. The eyes kept scouring the road ahead as it moved closer to Strongheart's camp, which was now almost in view. The eyes were well over eight feet above the road.

The predator was very careful where each foot went, and what body part touched overhanging and roadside branches. Stealth had provided success in the past and was imperative now, because the man in the camp was a known quantity. He knew what he was doing and was presenting the biggest challenge for the predator yet.

Rounding a house-sized rock by the trail, he could now see the camp, the fire, the sleeping figure under the blanket. Slowly; he must be patient, very patient. Inching forward.

Movement! His eyes twisted up and to the right. A large figure was diving at him from the top of a boulder, and before he could react, a giant, muscular shoulder slammed into his torso and sinewy arms wrapped around him. They hit the ground with a thud, stunning him, and he opened his eyes, feeling the razor-sharp blade of Strongheart's big knife against his throat. His black mask was pulled off, and he saw his big black Thoroughbred horse bolting away, totally unnerved by Strongheart's surprise ambush. He was panicked, unable to breathe, and every part of his body hurt from the fall off the horse and Joshua's vicious tackle. Scared to death, tears filled his eyes.

"Mr. Strongheart, it's me, Scottie!" he yelled in sheer panic. "Don't kill me, please!"

Joshua stood and jerked the teenaged boy up by the lapels with one hand. He dragged him to the fire and shoved him into a seating position. Strongheart gave out a low whistle, and Eagle soon came trotting up from the shadows of the road north of the camp.

Scottie gingerly touched his face as a small trickle of blood ran from one nostril, and his left eye was swelling shut from the impact of Strongheart's diving tackle from the top of the rock. He started crying.

Strongheart poured a cup of coffee for himself and growled, "Hush up! You took on a man's task, so face the consequences like a man!"

Scottie was shocked into silence. The sobs ceased. Strongheart had always been so gentle with him, kind and understanding, and his sharp admonition shook Scottie into immediate compliance.

It was just before noon the next day when the Fremont County sheriff heard a knock on his office door and said, "Come in."

Strongheart walked in holding Scottie by the scruff of the neck.

He plopped the teenaged boy down in a chair across from the sheriff and said, "Here is your monster, the phantom of Phantom Canyon. His big black Thoroughbred, Hero, which was a gift from me, is outside."

Joshua thought back to that day several years earlier after he busted the Indian Ring and took the leader's big black Thoroughbred. Strongheart had led it to the home of Scottie Middleton and his aunt.

Joshua had said simply, "Mount up."

The horse was so tall Scottie had trouble getting into the saddle, and his aunt had tears in her eyes.

Strongheart said, "A man needs a horse, not a pony. He's yours."

Scottie told him he would name him Hero after Strongheart.

* * *

The lawman surveyed the frightened young man in front of him dressed in all black. Joshua tossed the boy's black mask down on the desk. The sheriff shook his head in wonder and looked at Strongheart with a grin. How powerful was gossip? With no words, this had just told him volumes. A teenaged boy dressed in black on a big black horse was what had spawned the legend of the ten-foot-tall monster in Phantom Canyon. People, in the dark, saw parts of the black Thoroughbred and probably Scottie's head and shoulders usually hidden in shadow. Tracks of the horse in the vegetation-covered but rocky terrain away from the well-worn road would be obscure at best.

Joshua explained, "I fed him last night and this morning, but we did not discuss much. I wanted to hear his full story along with you."

The sheriff nodded and leaned forward, picking his teeth with a straw from the broom in the corner.

"Son, I wasn't sheriff then," the sheriff said, "but I was a deputy. Didn't you used to clean up for us around here a coupla years ago?"

"Yes, sir," Scottie said.

Scottie thought about what he had been through with Strongheart and felt ashamed. He had worked up his courage several years earlier and gone to the sheriff's office to meet the tall Pinkerton he had heard so much about. After meeting Joshua, the little boy reached into his trousers and pulled out a small leather bag. He opened it, and marbles rolled out onto the desk. He reached in and pulled out some change and held it out.

He said, "Mr. Strongheart, I saved me up some money and have four dollars here. I want to hire you to find the man who stole my pony Johnny Boy and get him back for me. Ma and Pa gave me Johnny Boy last Christmas, and it is all I have from them. That gang a men burnt our house down when they kilt Pa."

He had explained that his mother had died of consumption one year earlier, and now he lived with a very nice aunt and a very mean drunk for an uncle.

Impressed, Strongheart shook hands and agreed to hunt down the boy's pony and get it back for him if it was alive. The trail took him up to Denver and Aurora, but after some shooting, he recovered the pony Johnny Boy and brought him back.

Scottie thought about how impressed he was when Strongheart came to his house along the Arkansas River near the First Street Bridge. The Arkansas River was due west of Cañon City, where it churned its way through a rocky canyon for miles, dropped thousands of feet, and produced some of the largest and wildest whitewater rapids in the world. After it poured out of the Grand Canyon of the Arkansas, which was starting to be called the Royal Gorge, the whitewater rapids disappeared pretty much, but the water still rushed with more power than in most rivers in the West.

Seeing Scottie's place, Joshua rode up to the front of the modest home, dismounting, and Scottie rushed out of the house, grinning broadly. A middle-aged woman with a kindly but haggard face walked out, and Strongheart doffed his hat to her. She was followed by a staggering brute of a man who obviously had been drinking.

As Strongheart walked up to the group, he said, "You have a fine young man here in this nephew of yours. My name is Joshua Strongheart," and he tipped his hat brim again. This brought a big smile on her tired but pretty face.

Strongheart walked straight up to the uncle and said, "And you must be Dave."

The man started to say something, but his words were shut off when Joshua suddenly reached out and grabbed him, spinning him around. He then seized the back of the man's unkempt hair, then grabbed the waistline of his homespun trousers in his other hand, jerked up, and gave it a twist. Now holding Dave up on his tiptoes, he started marching him toward the river in a rapid manner. Reaching the river's edge, Strongheart pitched the drunk into the cold, glacial-fed water. The man went under and came up ten yards downstream gasping and flailing at the water while his family watched from the house in horror. Strongheart jogged along the river's edge and waded into the water at a shallower spot.

Joshua repeated this, dunking the man underwater several times and giving him very stern warnings about his future treatment of Scottie. It turned out that Dave actually straightened out after that and got a job as a guard at Old Max, the state penitentiary in Cañon City.

It was some time later that Strongheart showed up with the big black Thoroughbred as a gift for Scottie, who in turn gave the pony Johnny Boy to a little neighbor boy who was very poor.

Scottie told the sheriff the story about his relationship with the tall, handsome Pinkerton, adding that he wanted to be a Pinkerton someday.

Joshua shook his head. "Young man, you say you want to be a Pinkerton, so you go out after dark in Phantom Canyon and dress in black, scaring people, and are very, very lucky you never got your head blown off!"

The sheriff chimed in, "Not only that—do you have any idea how much jail time you are facing and how many crimes I can charge you with?"

Without letting up, Joshua added, "You were responsible for a man's death, and the deaths of his horses as well. This is very serious business, young man."

His now-changing voice breaking from low to high, Scottie started crying.

He said softly, "Yes, sir."

Strongheart did not change expression, frightening Scottie with the stern look on his face.

He said, "All right, young man. The sheriff heard about our background—now what is the story on you following and scaring people half to death? Also, dry up the tears. You are playing a man's game; act like a man."

"Yes, sir," Scottie said. "Sir, I want to be a Pinkerton agent like you so bad. I wanted to learn how to be sneaky, like you can be. I started following people in

Phantom Canyon, riding Hero there, seeing if I could put the sneak on them without anybody seeing me. The more I got away with it, I guess the cockier I got."

The sheriff looked at Strongheart, unseen by the lad, and gave him a wink and a grin. Joshua was being very tough on Scottie, but his heart was breaking for him. Scottie, in the meantime, was heartbroken, because he could tell that his hero was very disappointed in him. The teenager wondered if Joshua would even have anything to do with him after this.

Scottie knew how much Joshua respected total honesty, so he decided to be brutally honest.

He said, "I guess I got cocky when I started hearing stories about the big monster in Phantom Canyon, and I started thinking that was me. It really made me feel special, and I really didn't know I caused anybody to die, sir. Honest."

Strongheart said, "I'm surprised your aunt and uncle would let you out so late, and so far away. That's a good ten-mile ride from your place, almost."

Scottie looked down.

He said, "My aunt is in bed a lot, Mr. Strongheart. She cries a lot and has been sick some. My uncle left us, lost his job at the prison, and has taken up drinking again."

Joshua felt bad.

He said, "Where is your uncle?"

Scottie said, "He hangs out all the time at McClure's Saloon. I heard he is living in an old miner's cabin up north of town."

The sheriff stood up and looked over at Strongheart, waiting to follow his lead.

Joshua said, "Well, Sheriff, you have to figure out what charges you're going to levy on Scottie. Why don't you toss him in a cell so we can talk about it?"

"Good idea," the sheriff said, and grabbed Scottie's arm as tears welled up in the boy's eyes again.

He led him from the room, saying, "C'mon, youngster."

Strongheart heard him open and then shut and lock the door of a cell, and the sheriff walked back into his office, closing the door. He and Joshua immediately started chuckling.

The sheriff said, "I swear, Strongheart. You sure put the fear of the good Lord into him. I'll bet you he walks the straight and narrow the rest of his life. How long should we make him worry?"

Strongheart said, "Why don't you make us both fresh cups of coffee while he cools his heels and worries? You can tell me how your family has been and what is happening with your folks."

The sheriff winked and poured two steaming cups of coffee, handed one to Joshua, and sat down at his desk with his. They talked for a good twenty minutes while Scottie sweated bullets and choked back tears in his cell. He swore to himself he would never ever do anything to be put in a jail cell again if he got out of this somehow.

He thought about the last time he had seen his uncle.

The man came home drunk, and Scottie came in the door while his uncle Dave was rummaging through the cookie jar where Scottie's aunt kept her emergency money. She was pleading and rubbing a swelling red welt on her left temple.

"Please," Aunt Kathy pleaded. "We need that money for food, David!"

Scottie's voice had changed, and he had gotten much taller. He was becoming a young man, and this incident made him reach an important decision.

He ran over to his uncle and jerked him around, pointing and yelling, "Did you hit my aunt? Did you hit my aunt?"

Dave swung at the boy, but was extremely drunk, and his punch was looping and sloppy. Scottie ducked and hit Dave with a looping hook punch that caught him flush on the side of his mouth. Blood immediately streamed from his uncle's mouth as the drunk flew into the table and fell on the floor in a clatter of dishes and bowls. To add insult to injury, the table fell over sideways on the man, the edge of it gashing his forehead open.

Scottie grabbed the table and flung it aside, then pointed at his bleeding uncle. He was shaking, he was so angry—something that had never really happened before.

The boy said, "Uncle Dave, if you ever lay a hand on Aunt Kathy again, I will beat you within an inch of your life! Do you understand me, Uncle Dave? I mean it!"

Grumbling and rubbing his bloody face, the drunk

got up and staggered out the door, mumbling under his breath.

Scottie turned to see his aunt staring at him with awe and pride on her face and tears in her eyes.

She held Scottie and said softly, "Good riddance."

Now Scottie looked around the jail cell and shook his head, and tears welled up in his eyes.

In the office, Joshua walked toward the door, saying, "I may be back in a few minutes or a half an hour."

He was formulating a plan for Scottie, and he left the sheriff wondering what it might be as he watched Joshua walking a block down and entering McClure's Saloon.

Walking in, he heard someone say, "Howdy, Mr. Strongheart!"

He gave a wave and headed toward the corner where Scottie's uncle Dave was sitting, back to the door, very drunk, as usual. Strongheart reached down, grabbed him by the back of his lapel with his left hand, and grabbed the man's ear with his right hand, lifting him out of the chair and marching him toward the door.

Strongheart said, "Come on, Dave. We're taking a little walk."

Uncle Dave screamed in pain, his eyes slowly moving around while he tried to figure out what was going on. Strongheart marched him downhill the quarter of a mile to the fast-flowing, summer-swollen Arkansas River. Then he walked him a block up the river road west to the Fourth Street Bridge and out over the angry, raging watercourse, the drunken man arguing all the way. Several passersby followed the two out of sheer curiosity, and the word quickly went through the crowd that it was the famous Joshua Strongheart teaching somebody a lesson.

Joshua looked the drunken man in the eyes and said through gritted teeth, "What did I tell you would happen if I caught you drinking ever again?"

Uncle Dave's eyes opened wide in sheer panic as he protested, "Mr. Strongheart, I cain't swim!"

Joshua said, "Good time to learn."

He picked the man up by his neck and his hair and tossed him off the bridge like a rag doll. Screaming, Dave hit the water with a splash, and Strongheart walked fast back toward the sheriff's office without looking to see if the man was going to flail his way to a river bank or not. People in the crowd didn't seem to care, either, as they simultaneously applauded and laughed, watching Joshua walk away.

Minutes later, he was in the sheriff's office and sitting down to a new cup of coffee.

The sheriff looked at Strongheart and started chuckling.

He took a sip of his own coffee and said, "Pay his uncle a visit?"

Joshua grinned, saying, "If you want to ask him, Sheriff, I think you'll find him taking a leisurely swim down the Arkansas."

The lawman slapped his leg and started guffawing. He looked at the half-breed and shook his head, just roaring.

Joshua said, "I think I'd like to talk with the boy again."

The sheriff left the room, returning in a minute with Scottie. The young teenager's eyes were red-rimmed.

Strongheart said, "Have a seat," and Scottie sat down.

Strongheart said, "Did we get your attention, young man?"

Scottie sat up straight. "Mr. Strongheart, Sheriff, I give you both my word as a man, I will never, ever break the law in my life again. Never!"

Joshua said, "Well, the sheriff has agreed to place you under my care. I'm going to hire you as an assistant, but I will expect a day's work for a day's wages. Agreed?"

Scottie beamed. "Yes, sir. Thank you, sir. Thank you, Sheriff."

Strongheart said, "Very well, then. Right now, we are going to go have a talk with your aunt."

Scottie went out and placed his bridle on his horse while Joshua spoke briefly with the sheriff, they shook, and he left. A few minutes later, Eagle and Hero were trotting down the river road toward Scottie's house.

Strongheart escorted Scottie inside. His aunt was shocked that the tall hero actually came into their house.

Joshua removed his hat and said, "Nice to see you again, Kathy. Scottie and I need to have a chat with you if you have a few minutes."

She had been working on a patchwork quilt and started putting her materials away, saying, "Please,

Mr. Strongheart, have a seat. I just made some apple pie and put coffee on when I saw you riding up."

He sat at the modest table, looking around at the small, neat house.

Strongheart said, "Please, I told you before, call me Joshua."

There was a look of concern on her suntanned face. She sat down, the edges of her gingham cotton dress flowing out over both sides of the chair. She cut pie for Joshua, Scottie, and herself, then got up and grabbed the coffeepot. She poured herself and Joshua cups of coffee and finally sat down.

The Pinkerton waited and said, "Scottie has been a busy young man for several months and wants to tell you of his activities."

He looked at Scottie, who had tears welling up in his eyes. He did not want to worry or hurt his aunt and knew his actions had been very selfish. The young man told the story of the monster of Phantom Canyon he had inadvertently become. To Strongheart's pleasure, he did not excuse himself or try to soften what he had done. She sniffled and shook her head while the story was being told.

When he finished and apologized, she said, "What I want to know is how you were able to disappear and ride so far away and so far back without me knowing it. I feel like I have failed you, as I have always tried to maintain a watchful eye over you."

With this, she sobbed a little and tears welled up in Scottie's eyes again.

He said, "I think that was part of the thrill of it, Aunt Kathy. I would sneak out after you went to sleep, or some nights when you be crying alone. I could hear ya, and I knew you would cry yourself to sleep."

Her face turned bright crimson as she looked over at Strongheart.

In explanation, she said, "I am so glad he is gone, Joshua. He became so cruel with all his drinking. Scottie beat him up and protected me, and he has not come back since. Is it true what my neighbor told me?"

Joshua grinned.

Scottie said, "What did they say, Auntie?"

"They said that Joshua marched your uncle down all the way from McClure's Saloon to the Fourth Street Bridge and tossed him into the Arkansas River, and he almost drowned. He got pulled out down on Ninth Street."

Scottie laughed and said, "Is that true, Mr. Strongheart?"

Joshua said, "Well, Scottie, you heard me warn him what would happen if he drank again."

"Oh, I wish I could have seen that!" Scottie said.

Strongheart and Scottie each ate another piece of pie, while Scottie and Joshua both finished filling in all the details of Scottie's misadventures.

Joshua pulled some money out of his Levi's and handed that money to Scottie.

He said, "All right, young man, you are going to work for me, and I want to pay you an advance on your earnings. Do you know what that means?"

"No, sir," the lad answered.

Strongheart said, "There is one hundred dollars there. I am giving you some of your wages now so you can be prepared to work your fanny off for me without worrying about your aunt."

Tears in her eyes again, Kathy looked at Joshua and mouthed the words, "God bless you."

Scottie said, "I can't take this, sir. I never seen this much money in my life."

Strongheart said, "I'm the boss, so you do not argue with me. Just do what you're told. Also, learn how to speak correctly. It is 'I never saw,' not 'I never seen.'"

"Yes, sir," Scottie said. "Thank you, sir."

He turned and handed the money to his aunt, who immediately headed toward her cookie jar to put it away. She hugged Scottie tightly and mouthed another silent thank-you to Joshua.

She straightened up, saying, "Well, you have apologized, and I forgive you. Now it looks as though you are growing up earlier than you wanted to, but maybe that is a good thing, Scottie. I trust Mr. Strongheart implicitly, so if there are days or nights you are not here, I will know he is watching over you. So skedaddle, and be sure you give Mr. Strongheart more than a fair day's work for his very generous wages."

She walked over to Joshua and stood up on her

tiptoes, pulling his head down to give him a peck on his cheek.

"Thank you, Joshua," she said, and walked to her bedroom, hiding her new, glistening tears.

The pair left the house and saddled up.

From that day on, no matter how manly Scottie would become, his eyes would well up with tears at the slightest emotional trigger.

The overpayment advance of several months' pay was not a problem for the Pinkerton, who always carried extra money. Joshua was actually very wealthy, having been left a large inheritance from his mother and step-father. Her mercantile was worth a lot of money when she passed, and she had saved and invested wisely. She also had taught him to be thrifty, so he gladly accepted his wages and expense account from the Pinkerton Agency.

His stepfather had told him years before, "Find a job that you would do for free, then do your job the very best you can and save your money."

Although he rarely attended or was even in town to attend, Joshua even gave tithes to and was a member of the First United Presbyterian Church of Cañon City, which was located near his late fiancée's home at Seventh and Macon Streets. By 1902, it would be built into one of Colorado's oldest and most beautiful churches, but right then, it was still a very nice church and quite popular with local residents, and had been since 1862. There were also popular Baptist, Methodist, and Catholic churches in the town. Strongheart believed in some of the tenets of his father's religion of the Lakota, but was a Christian in his heart and main beliefs. To him, spirituality was a necessity for a warrior. In fact, with his father's people, it was empirically more important to be considered in favor with the Great Spirit than it was to be brave in battle. It was the same way with many other native nations.

6

EDUCATION

There was only one time that Joshua did not have extra money hidden on him, and that was the last time he drank and got into very serious trouble. As they rode, he thought about that experience. Joshua had been riding south from Montana Territory and decided to spend the night in a town, opting for Cheyenne. It had only been established in 1867, in what was Dakota Territory that would later become Wyoming Territory, but a newspaper editor had already dubbed it the "jewel of the plains" because it had grown so rapidly. Joshua remembered crossing Crow Creek and heading to the Cheyenne Social Club to wet down some of the prairie dust he had been swallowing for several days.

* * *

He blinked his eyes and felt dizzy. His head felt like he was spinning in a circle, and his tongue felt like there was fuzz on it. A sweet-sour flavor crept from his stomach into his mouth, and Joshua sat up quickly on his bunk, making everything worse. He looked in the corner and saw a waste bucket for his use, and he ran to it, emptying whatever might have been left in his stomach into it. His head pounded as if his horse were standing on it and trotting in place. Finally, he spotted a bucket with a bar of soap and towel nearby, and he crawled to it on hands and knees and dunked his head in and out of the bucket three times. His head cleared a little as he shook it like an old dog who had just crossed a creek.

He blinked his eyes and then rubbed his face with the towel, looking around. Joshua Strongheart was in a dark, dusty jail cell and could not, for the life of him, figure out how he got there. He only remembered crossing Crow Creek and that was all, and now he was in a cell.

Joshua and Scottie rode toward the Royal Gorge as he remembered the rest of that incident, which was never far from his mind.

The outer door opened with a loud, rusty squeak, and Joshua scrunched his shoulders up with the sound, which made his headache hurt worse. He had never seen a more beautiful woman in his life. Dark auburn, her hair hung all the way down to the small of her back, and it had a natural curl in it, the morning sun streaking through the window making it glisten like dewdrops. The classy full-length shiny green dress she wore could not hide the natural curves of her body, but what entranced him were the light hazel, almost yellow eyes. She smiled looking at him and walked right up to the bars. Hesitantly, he got to his feet and walked forward.

"The deputy said I could visit with you briefly," she said through full crimson lips.

Joshua knew this beauty was speaking to him as if they were close. Her body language showed it, but he had no idea what had transpired the night before, or nights before.

He said softly, "Hi," still wondering why he was here and what had happened.

"Oh, you poor thing," she cooed, "your eye is black, and you have a nasty cut on your cheekbone. I was certain those men were going to kill you. How can I ever thank you?"

He suddenly realized his left eye was almost swollen shut, and he winced as he touched his cheekbone.

"Well," he said, actually trying to access information, "they were awfully tough. Weren't they?"

"Them?" she said, throwing up her hands. "You almost killed all three of them."

Now Joshua was really concerned, and it was driving him crazy trying to figure out a missing piece of his history. Had he nearly killed someone? Did he use a gun, or his knife? What had started it? He made a silent promise to himself to never drink again. It seemed like every time he tried to drink, things like this just seemed to happen, even if he just planned on having a cold beer. He also knew he had made himself the same promise before, but now here he was again, wondering what he had done.

She suddenly pulled him forward, kissing him full on the lips, and the door burst open again.

A very large and sloppy-looking strawberry-headed deputy walked into the room, saying, "Time's up, ma'am."

She whispered, "Even though they were paying customers, I could not believe how you took exception to them touching me. You were such a gentleman, protecting my honor."

Joshua stepped back and sat down hard on his cot.

He smiled at her feebly, saying, "Sorry. Hangover. Are they okay, ma'am?"

She headed toward the door, saying, "Don't know, sweetie. Ask him. Thanks again," indicating the deputy.

Joshua gave the deputy a sheepish grin and said, "Did I hurt some men last night?"

"Naw," the deputy replied, and Joshua felt relief.

Then the jailer added, "More like half kilt 'em. Ya broke up Bugger Johnson's face bad, knocked out a lot a the teeth he had left, broke his jaw, smashed his nose. Lessee, Big Ed Thomas, ya snapped his arm like it was firewood. He screamed like a durn banshee. Then poor ole Lucifer Rhames. Took the doc most a the night to get him awake. He cain't remember what happened, neither."

The deputy shuffled toward the door, then stopped and scratched his ample beard stubble, chuckling.

He added, "In fact, Lucifer cain't remember any a this week or last, the doc said. His face looks like the walls of Black Canyon out yonder. Phew. Ya gave them lads a whippin', Injun. You are durned-shore rattler-mean when you git some rotgut in ya. Guess you will be going down to the Territorial Prison down ta Cañon City fer a long visit. Hope ya like eatin' hog slop."

Laughing at his own joke, he exited, leaving Joshua with his confused thoughts.

What troubled the hungover, mixed-up young man was that this had happened before when he drank. He could not remember at all what happened, and he obviously turned into a monster.

Joshua got up and paced back and forth across the cell, muttering to himself, "I can't trust myself. Even if I have a beer this seems to happen. I get drunk and get whiskey-mean."

He set his jaw and told himself he must have the red man's weakness for liquor, and he would never, ever drink again. No sooner had he made this solemn oath to himself than the outer door creaked open again and the strawberry-headed jailer walked in with the keys, followed by a well-dressed, middle-aged man in a tailored businessman's suit. Joshua could clearly see the handles of the pair of Colt Navy .36's the man wore under his suit coat.

It was Lucky, and Joshua moaned out loud, "Damn!"

The door was opened, and, startled, Joshua walked out unsteady on his feet.

Lucky waited until Joshua was given his weapons and they had walked out into the blinding sunlight, with Joshua squinting his eyes and not realizing he was moaning out loud.

"This weel never happen again," Lucky said with a slight French accent, his face red with anger. "I had to call een a favor with zee judge, and the three men you broke up were happy to get one hundred dollars each for zere injuries."

Joshua felt horrible.

He said, "I am very sorry, Lucky. I will pay Pinkerton Agency back for the three hundred dollars."

Lucky interrupted. "Zee Pinkerton Agency deed not pay it. Zey do not know about thees. I paid eet, and you weel pay eet back, and your five-hundred-dollar fee for damages I paid to zee judge. You weel pay eet back each paycheck, one hundred dollars at a time, to me."

Joshua said, "Thank you very much, Lucky. I mean it. I will pay back two hundred dollars out of each paycheck, and I will never get into that kind of scrape again. I will never take another drink the rest of my life."

His own words hit him suddenly, and he shivered, but he had given his word and that was that. If he dared ever break his word, he knew the ghost of Marshal Dan Trooper would come back to haunt him. The man's stern lessons had stuck, especially about keeping your word, and would remain with Joshua Strongheart all his days.

Then he thought to himself what a skinflint he had been as they walked along.

He said, "Lucky, I have money, plenty of it, in the bank in Denver. I will repay you within the week every penny. It is not necessary to deduct any from my paycheck."

Lucky said, "*Sacre bleu*, Joshua! If you have plenty of money, why do you work for zee Pinkerton Agency?"

Strongheart said, "Lucky, I have not been with you long, but this job is a career for me, not a job. I love the work and the potential for the future. I was left an inheritance, so I do not have to work. I simply do not want to sit in some parlor every day listening to piano recitals and poetry readings, or sit on a slow-moving horse gathering cattle for market on some big ranch. I am proud to be a Pinkerton agent."

Lucky said, "Eef you ever drink like zat again, you weel not be a Pinkerton agent anymore."

Strongheart said, "I give you my solemn oath, I will never taste alcohol again, ever."

Lucky knew how strongly Joshua felt about always keeping his word, and that did it for him.

Strongheart looked over at Scottie and thought about how his uncle had hurt the young lad with excessive drinking. He was so glad that he had been able to recognize his own weakness early on and do something about it.

"Where are we going, Mr. Strongheart?"

Joshua said, "This is your first day of training."

"Training?"

"Training," Joshua repeated. "You said you want to be a Pinkerton agent, right?"

"Yes, sir," Scottie said enthusiastically.

Strongheart said, "We'll start off with a new rule. You're what now, fourteen, fifteen years old?"

Scottie proudly said, "Fifteen, sir."

Joshua said, "In many tribes, you would be fighting in battles and stealing horses, and might even be married with kids. You want to be a man, we'll help you become one, if you can handle the training."

"I can," Scottie boasted proudly, although inside his stomach he could feel butterflies flying upside down and sideways in anticipation of what lay ahead.

They had ridden uphill for eight full miles and were now one thousand feet higher than the Arkansas River, which was flowing a mile to their left down through a magnificent Arkansas River canyon that would become world famous for its pristine beauty, thousand-foot sheer cliffs, and the winding, churning, angry whitewater rapids that ran the length of the canyon. Before dark, they were riding down a long, winding hill, and Scottie could see the Arkansas River down below them. The area had been called Parkdale. At the bottom of the hill, there was a bridge and they rode across the river.

Scottie looked to his left and watched the churning water as it plunged into the steep-walled canyon. Now they rode west through a valley with rocky ridges in every direction with the river to their right. Strongheart spotted a grove of trees near the river and headed toward it.

They rode in and dismounted, and Joshua said, "We'll camp here tonight. Make camp for us."

Scottie's mind raced. He did not know what to do. He first unsaddled the horses and put the saddles near an old campfire in the middle of the grove. Joshua sat down, grinning, and drank from his canteen. Scottie was doing the best he could trying to figure out how to prepare the campsite, but seemed a bit lost. His uncle Dave had never done anything but be abusive, and Scottie had not been old enough for his father to teach him much before his death.

Strongheart stood up and he said, "Scottie, stop for a minute. Look up through the trees at the sky. Can you see those storm clouds coming in from the west?"

Scottie said, "Yes, sir."

Joshua said, "We are probably getting rain tonight, so what should be your first priorities?"

Scottie answered hesitantly, "A fire and shelter?"

Strongheart said, "Correct, and also water. Throw the saddles on the horses, and we will head toward that ridge one mile to the west. We need to find an overhang with trees and vegetation nearby. We'll be right by the river, so we will have plenty of water."

Where he was looking was one mile west, where the river came out of another narrow, steep canyon, called Bighorn Sheep Canyon by the locals. That canyon had very high mountain ridges extending up on both sides of the river, with a set of railroad tracks going through the gorge and then along the north side of the churning, boiling whitewater river. For forty miles, herds of bighorn sheep could be seen along the river, and occasional fluffy white Rocky Mountain goats, as well. The canyon was inundated with more mountain lions per square mile than any other place in the United States, and cinnamon- and blond-phase black bears and grizzly bears roamed freely through the many gulches and ridges that ran on either side of the river to both the north and the south.

Strongheart found a spot along the south side of the raging current where there was a large rock overhang.

He showed this selection to Scottie and explained, "If you have rain or snow threatening, or even possible, you always want shelter. With the mountains we so often have around us, shelter is already created by nature. We have a rock overhang that juts out over us, so now we use rocks and dig if we need to make sure torrents of water won't come down the mountain and wash from the sides into our camp."

There were only a few spots where it could become flooded, and the pair made blocking fences with large rocks to route the water beyond the camp.

Finishing that, Strongheart said, "Now we need firewood, several dry logs and large branches, then smaller branches, and then squaw wood."

"I thought *squaw* was a bad word?" Scottie asked.

"No, that's a fairy tale, Scottie," Joshua responded.

"It's a good word for a woman. Do you know what squaw wood is?"

Scottie replied, "No, sir."

Strongheart said, "It is smaller, dry wood—twigs, small sticks—and pinecones that you can pick up, the small dead branches easily reached on the lower end of trees, and the sawdust-like wood you find at the base of trees. That is what you start a fire with. Sometimes, when you look for that, you will find old birds' nests that are dried out, and they make good tinder for starting a fire, too."

The two started gathering wood, and Scottie was very excited, because he did find an old bird's nest, which he proudly displayed for Strongheart. They gathered more wood, and Joshua showed Scottie how to start the fire using the bird's nest in the middle of a small teepee fire. That teepee fire was set up in the middle of a log cabin fire with larger logs going in both directions, overlapping each other, just like the construction of a log cabin. Joshua let Scottie do most of the construction of their fire and had him place rocks all around it. He cautioned him about not using rocks from the nearby rushing river, because they would sometimes contain pockets of water which could heat up, boil, and literally explode.

After getting a fire going, Strongheart pointed at the rock overhang, saying, "Now, this is important, especially when it is freezing cold: You want the heat from your fire to bounce off rocks like that and keep you much warmer. When you build a reflecting fire, you do not have to use as much firewood to stay warm. In the wintertime, you will appreciate that. Sometimes, I make camp in a grove of trees, and the trees dissipate or spread out your smoke, so your enemies do not see where you are as easily. In this case, the same thing happens with an overhang, especially when there is fog in the morning. People at a distance see the smoke from your fire going up the mountain, and it simply mixes in with the morning fog."

Scottie was amazed how this day had turned out. It had started so badly but was ending so wonderfully. He could not believe he was being trained by Joshua Strongheart on how to become a Pinkerton agent, but back at his house his aunt lay in bed crying and smiling. She knew that Joshua Strongheart was teaching her nephew how to become a man.

After dinner, Strongheart pointed at the fire and said, "See how we have a small fire but are warm as biscuits and gravy? That is because we have rocks reflecting its heat. There is an old saying, 'The stupid cowboy builds a large fire and burns on one side and freezes on the other, but the wise Indian builds a small fire and stays warm all over.'"

Scottie took a sip of hot cocoa and said, "That is neat, Mr. Strongheart."

Joshua corrected, "We are saddle partners and work together. Call me Joshua."

Scottie's chest puffed out a little as he smiled.

Strongheart said, "If you need a fast fire, you build that teepee fire we built earlier and you put good dry tinder or a bird's nest or crumpled-up paper in the center to start it. Also, always remember that a fire has to breathe, like humans, so always have spaces between logs and sticks."

"Yes, sir."

Joshua put a large log on the fire, then lay down on his tarp over pine boughs, his head on the saddle.

He said, "We have to get up early. Going to get some shut-eye."

Scottie said awkwardly, "What about me, Joshua?"

Strongheart closed his eyes and replied, "Suit yourself. A man should do what he likes."

Scottie beamed, and then said, "What about keeping watch?"

Strongheart responded, "Not here. The horses will let us know if anybody approaches. There will be times you are on alert, but not here, not now."

Scottie opened his eyes and creaked his neck. He could smell fresh-brewed coffee on the fire, and the sun was lighting the sky back in the direction of Cañon City, now eleven miles east and on the other side of the foothill that rose a mile above the Arkansas River, forming the Royal Gorge. He sat up and saw that Eagle was saddled and Joshua was eating breakfast. Scottie shook his head, realizing he had fallen asleep quite some time after Joshua the night before. He had slept leaning against a stump and was now stiff and sore. He noticed Joshua was clean—his hair was glistening, and he apparently had bathed—and was now clothed and ready to ride.

Strongheart said, "If you're going to be my saddle partner, you keep clean. Run to the river's edge, brush your teeth, and take a quick bath."

He tossed Scottie a bar of soap.

Scottie said, "Yes, sir, but how do I dry off?"

Strongheart said, "I carry my own towel in my saddle roll. Guess you will need to use leaves and the sun."

Scottie said, "What about breakfast?"

Joshua grinned, saying, "You slept instead. Hope it was worth it."

Scottie felt disappointment in himself. He turned toward the river and trotted off, following the same game trail Strongheart had used an hour earlier. The only problem was, when Joshua had bathed in the icy cold water, there had been no outside visitors. Now there was one.

Scottie was naked and carefully walking along the rocks and boulders alongside the very powerful, angry, churning river roaring past him. He made his way around a large green bush growing between two boulders on the river's edge, and came face-to-face with a large cinnamon-and-blond-colored black bear holding a dead young bighorn sheep in its mouth. Scottie and the bear both froze, both shocked, and the bear dropped the bighorn, growled, and popped its teeth.

Normally, black bears were not a menace to man, and they were usually nocturnal and extremely shy. Even a small barking dog could ofttimes send one scampering away. However, if a person got in close proximity to a sow bear with cubs, or, like in this case, seemed to be a threat to a bear's meal, then the bear could become a vicious killing machine. And in this case, it happened to be a very large boar bear with a freshly killed yearling bighorn sheep.

The bear, ears laid back, took a step forward, and the nude young teenager stepped back. His bladder let go, and he felt the warm liquid running down the inside of his leg. He had never been this scared in his whole life, except when Strongheart had knocked him out of the saddle in Phantom Canyon. He could barely breathe, his legs were shaking and weak, his brain felt like it was filled with Aunt Kathy's oatmeal, and his heart was pounding hard in both ears. He tried to think and tried to keep himself calm.

Then he thought, "What would Strongheart do?"

He kept backing away, trying to look nonthreatening, and his mind raced to try to remember various tips Strongheart had given him. Several times, he could tell the big beast's muscles were bunching up as it prepared to make a charge; its relatively tiny ears were laid back on its head.

Suddenly, he heard Joshua's voice. "Scottie, do not

run, whatever you do. Keep facing the bear and walk backward very slowly. Do not look the bear in the eyes. Just talk softly to the bear while you walk backward and tell him you did not mean to invade his territory, or whatever you want to say. If he charges, I will shoot him, but let's try to avoid that."

Scottie kept slowly walking backward, and the bear inched forward.

Scottie remembered not to look into the bruin's eyes. Besides this incident, he had been told by Strongheart before that looking into a boar bear's eyes was one of the surest ways to get the bear to charge. He could hardly breathe as he watched the big bruin inch forward as he inched backward. He was so relieved to know that Joshua was there, obviously covering him, but the presence of the bear was so unnerving. The bear suddenly stood up on his hind legs and sniffed the wind while popping his teeth and swinging his head from side to side.

Just as he thought his knees would give way under him, he saw a blast of dirt and dust go flying up a few feet in front of the bear, and at the same time, he heard the loud blast of the tall Pinkerton's Colt Peacemaker.

Then Strongheart followed this immediately with a loud yell. "Get out of here, Brother Bear!"

That did the trick; the bear did not run, but it turned, paused and looked back slowly, and then trotted away around the bend of the river.

Scottie's legs suddenly felt like wilting celery stalks and gave way under him. He dropped down in place, and Strongheart rode up from behind him on Eagle. Joshua grinned softly and stuck his arm down. Scottie grabbed his sinewy forearm, and the Pinkerton swung the lad up behind him on the big horse.

Minutes later, Scottie was mounted, and the two headed across the short valley for one-half mile to Copper Gulch Stage Road. From there, they started up the familiar road, heading south. Strongheart was taking Scottie to an area where he had almost lost his own life to a large grizzly and in several gunfights, near Lookout Mountain and across the northern end of the Wet Mountain Valley from the majestic Sangre de Cristo range.

They rode for miles in the high-steeped ridge gulch, giant boulders looming up between the cedars, piñons, and scrub oaks along the way as the two riders climbed all day from an elevation approximately a mile high to around eight thousand feet. Turning on Copper Gulch Stage Road, which had held many previous adventures for Strongheart, Scottie looked five to ten miles to his left at the towering Sangre de Cristo range, stretching as far as he could see to the south and blending in perfectly in the north with the Collegiate Range. He did not even know how many of the beautiful snowcapped peaks were over fourteen thousand feet in height, but there were dozens of the white-topped sentinels stretching up into the endless blue, cloudless sky. Scottie had seldom seen these majesties, even from a distance, yet here they were, less than a full day's ride from Cañon City, witnessing their humbling presence.

Strongheart had Scottie putting together their camp and had plans before dark. Every time he slowed down, like teenagers are wont to do, Joshua was there to put a verbal boot up his behind, motivating him into action.

He lectured, "Scottie, whenever you are supposed to do any kind of job, no matter what you are paid or not paid, work so fast, so hard, and so completely that you know that person will beg you to come back and work for them again."

"Yes, sir," Scottie said, while stacking another large armload of dry wood next to the circular, rock-lined cooking fire.

Strongheart then walked over to his saddlebags and returned carrying a worn belt and holster, its loops filled with .44 rounds. He pulled the pistol out and handed it to Scottie. Scottie took it and looked at it admiringly. Joshua quickly yanked it out of his hand.

He explained, "Lesson one, always check and clear any weapon the second it is handed to you. Never take anybody's word that it is or is not loaded. Always check it with your own eyes."

Scottie was excited, and he said, "Yes, sir. Is this your extra gun?"

"No, it's yours," Strongheart said, "if you're man enough to handle it. That is called a Russian .44, and it is a man-sized gun. Is it too big for you?"

Scottie puffed his chest out and said, "No, sir. Thank you so much. Thank you very much."

Strongheart said, "You're welcome, but that is with

the conviction that you will always use it as a tool, as an instrument for good. Become proficient, so nobody innocent can get hurt because you cannot hit what you are shooting, and so that no animal suffers because you cannot shoot straight. Fair enough?"

Scottie was beaming. "Yes, sir!"

Joshua said, "Okay, put on the holster."

The young man did so, and Joshua showed him how to wear it comfortably and effectively. Then he took the pistol from Scottie and tucked it into the back of his own waistband with the simple instructions, "Follow me and, with your right hand in the holster, when I say the name of an object we can see, pull your hand up like you drew your pistol and point at that object with your finger."

As they walked through the trees, Joshua would say, "Broken branch," "Yellow flower," "Brown rock," and after ten times of Scottie drawing his imaginary pistol at these objects, Joshua stopped.

He said, "Now we are going into that next patch of woods across the meadow. This time when you draw and point, I want you to stop, hold your hand and finger still, and kneel down and aim right along your finger."

They walked through the trees and again Joshua called out objects. Scottie drew his imaginary pistol and knelt down and aimed along the top of his finger, and he saw that he was pointing directly at the object every single time.

He mentioned this to Strongheart and Joshua replied,

"Scottie, when we point, even if we hold our hands down at waist level, we always point straight at the object we are looking at. That is normal. Tomorrow, you will be doing it with your gun, unloaded. You want to learn to point, not aim."

"That is amazing!" Scottie said.

They started walking back toward their campsite, and Joshua handed Scottie's pistol to him. The young man immediately put it in his holster.

Strongheart stopped. Scottie knew something was wrong. Joshua looked around and found a good-sized rock that weighed maybe fifty pounds. He removed the gun from Scottie's holster and immediately checked it and cleared it.

He handed the rock to Scottie and said, "Carry it. It better not touch the ground."

Scottie's heart sank as he tried to keep up with the seemingly angry Pinkerton agent. In actuality, Joshua was grinning to himself as he walked in front of the young man. His discipline of Scottie was nothing compared to that his stepfather, Marshal Dan Trooper, gave to him. As he walked, Strongheart daydreamed, thinking back to an early memory.

Dan was an incredible shot with pistol or rifle. He started Joshua when he was small and taught him first how to shoot a long gun. He learned to shoot with an

1860 Henry .44 repeater, and his stepdad gave it to him when he turned twelve years old.

It was a Saturday morning, and Dan handed him the rifle with two bullets and an admonition. "Boy, you have two bullets. One is for emergency. The other is for a deer, turkey, antelope, elk, or bear. We need meat. Your ma packed you some fixings. Saddle up old Beau and get us meat. Come back when you have it."

"Yes, sir," Joshua said, and walked away from the grim-faced lawman, his shoulders back and chest puffed out.

It was scary when he had to spend that night in the woods by himself, but he thought of his ancestry and what a mighty warrior his father had been. He finally tracked down a small doe, shot her, field dressed her, and returned home proud. Dan was proud of him, very proud, but would not show it. His mother was bursting with pride.

Dan said, "Good. Clean your rifle and sharpen your knife?"

"Yes, sir," came the quick reply.

"Good," the marshal said. "Give me the second bullet."

Joshua got a sheepish look. "I can't, sir."

"Why not?"

Joshua replied, "I had to use both bullets. I missed with the first shot."

"I told you the second bullet was for emergencies,"

Dan said. "What if you ran into a grizzly or a band of Crows on your way back?"

He did not wait for an answer, but said, "Out to the shed, Joshua," grabbing the leather razor strop off the wall.

Before he gave him his swats, he said, "If you point and cock a gun at an animal or a person, son, you shoot, and you do not miss. One bullet, one hit."

Joshua Strongheart never forgot those words—"One bullet, one hit"—and subconsciously touched his rear end every time he recalled the quote.

Dan never said words of sentiment or affection, nor did he praise Joshua, but a look of approval from him made Joshua's day. The man sure did teach the young lad how to fight with his hands and his pistol and rifle, but more importantly, with his head.

Strongheart thought about how relatively easy he was being on Scottie, and Scottie was thinking about how heavy the rock was and how ashamed of himself he was. Joshua gave him the rock and warning, but said nothing else. He did not need to. Scottie was beating himself up, because he had already ignored rule number one. He had not checked and cleared his weapon when Joshua handed it to him. He told himself that he would never, ever forget that again.

When they got back to the camp, Strongheart told Scottie he could put the rock down. Scottie dropped it and was so relieved. He realized he was drenched with sweat and both of his arms and his right shoulder were aching like crazy. The teenager slept the sleep of the dead and awakened in the morning with his arm really aching. He spent several days in the mountain camp, learning how to shoot his new weapon, draw, fire, and hit the target he was aiming at.

On the fifth day, the two were practicing quick draw, and Strongheart stood to Scottie's left front, very close. It made Scottie uncomfortable. He looked at the target Strongheart had selected, waiting to draw and fire if his mentor yelled, "Draw!"

Joshua explained, "Scottie, if you plan to be a Pinkerton or a lawman, you have to realize that at some point you might get shot. If you do, it is especially important that you still draw, fire, and hit the man who is trying to kill you."

Scottie said, "Yes, sir."

Suddenly, Strongheart yelled, "Draw!"

Scottie drew immediately and suddenly Strongheart's fist hit him hard in the stomach, throwing him backward and knocking the wind out of him while folding him like a suitcase. He lay on the ground, unable to regain his breath, and was starting to panic. He heard Joshua yelling, "Fire! Fire!" and drew and shot twice, hitting the knot on the tree Strongheart selected with both rounds. Then he holstered his gun and tried hard to gain his breath.

Joshua snarled, "Reload immediately!"

Still panicking as he tried to breathe, Scottie ejected his two empty shells and put two more into the revolver.

His eyes were wide open in sheer panic, and Strongheart felt for him. He'd had the wind knocked out of him before and that panicky feeling was no fun, but he had to be a harsh taskmaster. This was very serious business.

He quickly said, "Stand up fast, even if you're scared."

Scottie complied, and Joshua said, "Now jump up in the air and come down hard on your heels with your legs straight."

Scottie jumped up and came down with a jarring thud, knees locked, and landed on his heels. He was amazed! He could breathe! Just a second before, he was almost ready to cry, he was so panicked.

Joshua clapped him on the shoulder with pride and said, "Come look at this."

They walked to the tree with the knot that Joshua had picked out as a target. He pulled out a silver dollar and placed it over the two bullet holes that were almost dead center in the knot. The coin covered both holes. Scottie looked at it, and Joshua handed him the silver dollar.

He said, "Keep this dollar always and remember what you did. Shooting like that can keep you alive."

Scottie's shoulders went back, and his chin jutted out a little. His whole body ached from the work and tough training Strongheart had been giving him this week, but he felt like he was starting to become a man. He touched his stomach. It was sore where he had gotten punched, but he knew a bullet in the gut could make him a lot more sore, and he would remember well this new lesson.

There was a small herd of pronghorns that ran back and forth between these large scattered patches of high-mountain meadows. The pair was walking back to camp and rounded the bend of one patch of trees and came upon ten pronghorns bedded down in the mountain grasses twenty yards away. The herd jumped up and five started running, while the other five stared at the two in shock, ready to flee. Strongheart drew, fanning his gun, and shot a small antelope as the others fled. It rolled over once and was dead.

They walked toward the downed animal and Joshua said, "Have you ever eaten antelope?"

Scottie said, "No, sir."

The tall Pinkerton agent said, "It is the best eating there is outside of mountain lion."

"Mountain lion?" Scottie said.

Joshua replied, "Yes. Stop and think about it. They only eat deer just about, and are very finicky. After a few days they leave it to bears or coyotes and go on and kill another one. Mountain lion is delicious."

They arrived at the young antelope's body. Joshua knelt down, drawing out his knife. He closed his eyes.

Scottie said, "Were you praying?"

"Sort of," Joshua explained. "You know, I am half Sioux, so when I was your age, I learned to speak to an animal's spirit after I have killed it, to thank it for providing me with food, and to tell it I will not waste any of its body."

Scottie thought about this a minute and was impressed.

He said, "Gosh. Mr. Strongheart, I . . ."

Joshua said, "Call me Joshua, not *Mister*."

"Yes, sir," the teen said. "I never thought of anything like that. That is kinda neat."

Strongheart replied, "Well, I think the important message to get from that is to never kill an animal just to kill. Kill them for food and do not waste any of the meat, and use the hide and antlers wherever and whenever you can."

The lad had learned yet another lesson this day.

Strongheart quickly and efficiently field dressed the pronghorn and said, "Okay, son. Pick it up and let's take it back to camp. We will eat well tonight and relax. Tomorrow, we'll head back to Cañon City."

Joshua made them a delicious meal and both had steaming cups of coffee. The teenaged young man could not believe how good the antelope tasted. He felt it was probably the best meat he had ever eaten, although his Aunt Kathy's meatloaf was a close second.

While they ate apple cobbler Strongheart made with flour and apple slices Aunt Kathy had given him and drank coffee, Scottie said, "Mister, I mean, Joshua, do you know any neat stories from the Injuns?"

Strongheart finished his cobbler, took a long sip of

coffee, and said, "I'll tell you in the manner of the way my father's people tell a story. There was a young Lakota boy named Dancing Hare, and his first cousin and best friend was named Boy Who Climbs Trees. Dancing Hare and Boy Who Climbs Trees were both very adventurous, and both were students at the Mission School. While attending the school, Dancing Hare became very excited about the white man he met, who was called a missionary. He liked what the man spoke about, and what the missionary said made perfect sense to him. After some months, Dancing Hare became a Christian, but his cousin and best friend, Boy Who Climbs Trees, remained true to his tribal beliefs and was indeed a true follower of Wakan Tanka, the Great Mystery.

"The religion of choice did not matter to each boy, and they respected each other's differences and opinions. What they really enjoyed more than anything was adventure. They could not wait to grow and hunt game for the family circles and fight in battles and count coup. Both hoped someday to become Dog Soldiers, the best of the best warriors in their tribe."

"What does *count coup* mean?" Scottie interjected.

Joshua smiled and said, "To make it simple, with my father's people, after touching a live enemy in battle or after some heroic deed is performed, like hunting and killing a grizzly bear, that is considered a battle honor. It is called counting coup. When you count coup, or perform a courageous act, you are awarded an eagle feather."

"Oh," the lad replied enthusiastically.

Strongheart continued with his story. "There was one major difference, though, and that was that Dancing Hare always believed in winning and would never admit defeat. Once, when wrestling with Fights the Badger, he would not give in when put in a painful hold and actually had two of his fingers broken, but would not quit and would not cry. Boy Who Climbs Trees, however, would give in easily in games and wanted to give up and do something else if he started losing.

"One day, the two boys decided to hunt coyotes far away from the safety of the tribal circle of teepees, their neighborhood. Dancing Hare, while they moved through a wooded draw, heard a strange noise and held up his hand. Then they saw them, a band of Pawnees wearing war paint and carrying many weapons. The boys were afraid and knew they must hide in a safe place, but where?

"Boy Who Climbs Trees said, 'We will be killed or captured!'

"Dancing Hare said, 'No, we will not. Do not give up so easily,' but while he ran, he prayed harder than ever before.

"Finally, he spotted a cave ahead and ran into it, followed by his whimpering friend. Dancing Hare discovered another cave entrance. It was actually shaped like a horseshoe, with two holes opening in the side of a draw. They hid inside and saw the Pawnee war party far off, studying their tracks, which they had tried to hide.

"Then they saw a mighty bear startled by all the commotion run out of the trees and straight toward them. It headed right at the cave, and Boy Who Climbs Trees yelled, 'Run! He will eat us!'

"Dancing Hare said, 'No, stay put and do not move. If you run, the Pawnees will surely catch you.'

"The bear ran into the cave and turned to face in the direction of the danger behind him. He lay down. At the same time, crying, Boy Who Climbs Trees ran as fast as he could out the other cave entrance. Dancing Hare saw him get captured almost immediately by the band of Pawnees. They looked at the cave entrance, but the leader said they should not bother the mighty bear they saw run into it, or they might be killed. They rode off with their captive tied and bound.

"All good Lakotas bathed often and would keep their hair and skin shiny with bear grease made from bear fat. This smell kept the mighty grizzly calm in the cave, and he did not smell Dancing Hare and did not look around and see Dancing Hare. A few minutes after the Pawnees rode away, the grizzly emerged and ambled away toward the trees.

"Hours later, scared but safe, Dancing Hare trotted toward his village, but looked up at the sky and smiled. He knew then that what many like his cousin Boy Who Climbs Trees would see as nothing but a bad thing turned out to actually be an answer to a prayer, but dressed as something scary. The rest of his life, he would always look for the good news hiding inside the bad news. Now he would summon the Dog Soldiers to go and rescue his cousin.

"In other words, Scottie, always find something good in any problem you are faced with, and always decide to survive any obstacle."

Scottie poured himself another cup of coffee and said, "That sure was a neat story. You have any more of them?"

Strongheart grinned and said, "In time."

7

GUNFIGHTERS

By dark the next day, they were back in Cañon City, and Scottie was very relieved to see he was in good shape, although he had a few nicks and bruises showing. More obvious than injuries, though, was the Russian .44 six-shooter he was wearing. His aunt offered Joshua a nice hot dinner, but he refused and went on to the Hot Springs Hotel to relax and take a nice soothing mineral bath that night and the next morning. The next day, he would ride to his modest home south of town in the area called Lincoln Park, but he loved to go to the Hot Springs Hotel at the mouth of the Royal Gorge and had been going there ever since his first days in Cañon City.

The Hot Springs Hotel was at the very west end of River Drive and had a footbridge that crossed the

Arkansas River to the north side of the river where the railroad tracks ran. Passengers could depart and cross the footbridge to the hotel. Directly to the west of the hotel was the mouth of Grape Creek, which ran for well over twenty miles to the Silver Cliff area and the new town of Westcliffe in the Wet Mountain Valley. Beyond it was the east entrance of the Royal Gorge, which had sheer rock walls rising straight up to over 1,100 feet in some places, and it ran for eight miles to Parkdale.

It was daybreak, and Strongheart was up and ready to head to the hot spring when he heard gunshots coming out of the gorge. With the sound of the rapids, he thought this was unusual, but with the solid rock walls and narrow canyon, it was understandable. After soaking up the warmth into his muscular body, he dressed and decided on a leisurely breakfast in the hotel dining room.

Strongheart was enjoying a plate of eggs, steak, potatoes, sliced tomatoes, coffee, and grape juice, followed by rhubarb pie and several cups of hot coffee. He was really savoring this meal after several days up in the mountains eating over a campfire.

Two men walked in, both wearing business suits, picking a table in the far corner of the room. One, wearing a gray derby tilted to the right, looked up at Strongheart, and Joshua felt the man had some of the most piercing, lightest blue eyes he had seen. He wore a full, thick mustache waxed to points at the ends.

The man with him was very slight and pale, and very

sickly looking. He had an even longer mustache, but his, too, came to points at the drooping ends. Early into their conversation, he had a series of coughing fits, but seemed to recover well.

It was he who spoke across the room to Strongheart, with a deep Southern drawl to his voice.

"Suh," he said, "since we all have enjoyed differing positions in the field of law enforcement, why don't you join us for some light conversation?"

Strongheart smiled and nodded and carried his plate and coffee cup to the table, along with his silverware. He sat down across from the sickly one.

Smiling broadly, he asked, "How would you know I have anything to do with law enforcement, sir?"

"Good question indeed, suh," the slight man answered. "It is quite obvious you are the very noted half-breed Pinkerton agent who goes by the name of Strongheart. This gentleman is mah friend Bat Masterson, a lawman of some sterling repute, suh."

Strongheart nodded at Bat and extended his hand.

The slight speaker then said, "I must say, both of you have fine reputations, not only as shootists, but as exceptional lawmen as well."

Strongheart said, "Are you a lawman, sir?"

The sickly man replied, "Nah, I am a sporting man, but for many years practiced the art of dentistry."

Strongheart grinned, extending his hand again, saying, "Doc Holliday?"

"Indeed, suh," he replied. "So, knowing mah name,

you know that I have become an expert of law enforcement operations by nature of the fact that I have been the subject of keen interest by so many lawmen over the years."

Strongheart chuckled.

Doc Holliday looked over at Bat and said, "Besides killing a demon who stood over two meters tall, and a giant grizzly that was attempting to eat him, this young man, Bat, had a gunfight a few miles from here and killed quite a few men. However, my friend, his heroics resulted in enough bullet holes in his own skin that he could have well been used to water some of the beautiful flowers we have seen around this stately establishment."

Bat and Joshua chuckled.

Doc added, "On top of that, he hunted down a gang of ne'er-do-wells who stole the wedding ring of a young beautiful widow and hunted each one down until he was able to secure her wedding ring and return it to her, for one reason only: He had given his word that he would."

Strongheart said, "Do you embarrass everybody that you first meet, Doc?"

Doc Holliday replied, "No, suh, only the ones I have respect for."

He tipped his hat to Joshua.

Joshua said, "Doc, I cannot believe you know that much about me, yet we have never met."

"I beg to differ, suh," Doc Holliday said. "We did meet indeed, several years ago."

"What?" Strongheart asked. "I would surely remember that, Doc!"

"Well, young man," the gunfighter and gambler responded, "you seem to have been a bit indisposed at the time."

Joshua was certainly puzzled now.

He asked, "When was this?"

Looking at Masterson, the retired dentist said, "You see, Bat, my new friend Strongheart here and I have a very dear mutual friend who lives due west of here by the name of Zachariah Banta. He took me to visit poor Mr. Strongheart in a Denver hospital while he lay motionless for days, the result of a very malevolent disagreement with a rather humongous-sized silvertip grizzly bear possessing the disposition of a knife-wielding prostitute I was unfortunately acquainted with in Durango."

Strongheart said, "I swear! Zach Banta is friends with everybody. He brought you to see me in the hospital when I was knocked out cold?"

Doc tipped his hat again and coughed, a little blood and spittle landing on his chin. He wiped it quickly with a handkerchief.

A waiter walked up and took Joshua's order for some more pie and poured more coffee for the two gunfighters.

Strongheart waited for him to walk away and said, "So what brings you two gentlemen to this part of the country?"

"Well, Joshua," Bat said, "not *what*, but *who*. We were hired to come here to help out the Atchison, Topeka and Santa Fe Railway. You know, they have had a squabble going on with the Denver and Rio Grande Railroad about laying a line through the Royal Gorge here and have been fighting over putting a line over Raton Pass down just across the border."

The Pinkerton said, "So, who at the railroad actually hired you?"

Doc Holliday said, "Well, suh, we just met with railroad officials, but we were first invited here by a gentleman named V. R. Clinton, who owns quite a spread in the south end of the Wet Mountain Valley and has many properties here and there."

Strongheart said, "I never met him. What's he look like?"

Bat said, "That's just the thing, Strongheart. We never met him. He sent for us, and some slingers met us in Pueblo, put us in a hotel there, and gave us handsome sums of money as a deposit on our services."

Joshua knew what services he meant. The man bought their guns.

Doc Holliday said, "I did not much care for his ramrod, a large, disagreeable gent named Big Mouth Schwinn. Please, Mr. Strongheart, don't even ask, suh, how he got the name Big Mouth."

Joshua chuckled while taking a bite of pie.

Doc went on. "He fancies himself a shootist, but like a typical tin horn, has notches carved on his pistol grips."

Bat said, "Doc, you want to take that walk while he eats his pie?"

Doc Holliday nodded, and both men stood.

Bat said, "If you'll excuse us a few minutes. We will let you enjoy your pie and coffee, and we had planned to just walk down here by the river and take a look at the mouth of the Royal Gorge."

"Sure," Joshua said.

As he watched the two walk out along the riverbank, he thought about how fortuitous it was that their paths had crossed. Both were very famous at the time and would, in later years, became legends of the Old West. Both were very colorful characters, as was Joshua Strongheart, but each in his own way.

Actually, the railroad wanted to hire Bat Masterson to assemble a gang, and he immediately mentioned Doc Holliday, so they asked him to hire the former dentist. Besides Doc, Bat had already contacted Dave Rudabaugh, Ben Thompson, and Mysterious Dave Mather, as well as about seventy others, for his gang. This, however, was all based on the initial contact from V. R. Clinton, who said he was representing the Atchison, Topeka and Santa Fe Railway.

Bat was a lawman and gunfighter from Kansas who worked with and was a good friend of Wyatt Earp. He was born in Canada on November 26, 1853, but moved with his family south. When he was around twenty years old, Bat and his brother started working as buffalo hide hunters, and Bat also worked as a cavalry scout. After that, he became a lawman in Kansas, where he and Wyatt Earp and Doc Holliday became friends. His brother was shot and killed in Kansas and died in Bat's arms.

So now what would become known as the "Colorado Railroad War," or the "Royal Gorge Railroad War," was actually already being fought in small squabbles and skirmishes and in court between the Atchison, Topeka and Santa Fe Railway and the smaller Denver and Rio Grande company. Actually, in 1878, the Atchison, Topeka and Santa Fe was competing against the Denver and Rio Grande to put the first line through Raton Pass. Both railroads had lines to Trinidad in southernmost Colorado, and the pass was the only access to continue on to New Mexico. Unlike many of the Rocky Mountain passes, Raton Pass actually barely rose much higher than Trinidad, but the area became very wooded and was teeming with elk, bears, and mule deer. Above and below that area, the terrain was more semiarid, with a lot of small hills covered with sagebrush, some small scrub oaks, and typical vegetation for southern Colorado. Directly to the west, the Sangre de Cristo mountain range, which was twenty miles or so south and west of where Strongheart was, was much closer to Raton Pass, which actually went through the outstretched eastern foothills of the range that extended into New Mexico.

Because of the Atchison, Topeka and Santa Fe hiring Bat Masterson in 1878, and hiring many other shootists, the Denver and Rio Grande was forced to give up the fight over Raton Pass to them. Then, in 1879, a silver strike in Leadville at the headwaters of the mighty Arkansas River, up above ten thousand feet in elevation, renewed the rivalry. Both companies were competing to put their line through the magnificent Royal Gorge. The Denver and Rio Grande hired a large band of gunfighters, too.

First using V. R. Clinton, in March of 1879, the railroad hired Bat Masterson to put together his large group of gunmen. This was when he brought in Doc and the others. Strongheart sipped his coffee and thought about the slender gambler and gunfighter.

When John—Doc's given name—was a teenager growing up in Georgia, his mother died of consumption, which was actually tuberculosis. His father remarried very shortly after, and Doc's life was turned upside down. He developed quite a temper. He also was close to his adopted Mexican brother, who came down with tuberculosis, and after a few years, Doc did, too.

He attended the Pennsylvania College of Dental Surgery, graduating in 1872, and opened his dental practice in Atlanta and had a few shooting scrapes with nobody getting hurt. Doc consulted a number of doctors and was told he had only a short time to live and was strongly encouraged to move out West to a drier climate. In October 1873, Doc Holliday moved to Dallas, Texas, and spent some time there. However, he continued to practice his quick draw and with his knife and still possessed his wicked temper, so he had a few shooting scrapes.

Just a few steps ahead of Texas Rangers, soldiers, and lawmen, he moved to Colorado in 1876 after several stops in Texas and several dead bodies. He lived in Pueblo, Leadville, Georgetown, and Central City, leaving three more bodies in those cities. The fact that he was dying gave him an almost suicidal bent when it came to gunfights. Because of his high intelligence, the doctor was a natural at card games and figuring out betting odds. He was also a very good dresser and, when he was not in shootouts, really conducted himself as a refined Southern gentlemen in his speech and mannerisms. All these factors made Doc Holliday a very colorful character with a rapidly growing reputation in the West as a shootist not to be challenged or trifled with.

The two gunfighters returned to the dining room and rejoined Strongheart, drinking a final cup of black coffee. They walked with him toward the door.

"Beautiful country around here," Bat said, making small talk.

Joshua replied, "I have some bad memories here, but bought a small spread, mainly because I love the climate and have friends here. We get sunshine almost every day all year long and hardly any snow in the winter—not like the snow up in the mountains around here or north or west."

Doc said, "Suh, we need to be headin' back to Pueblo.

I assume your business has not picked a side in this railroad skirmish?"

Strongheart said, "Not that I know of. Haven't heard."

"Well, suh, I certainly hope they do not side with the Denver and Rio Grande. I like you and respect you, Joshua Strongheart, and I certainly do not wish to meet you in a hostile disagreement."

Bat said, "I agree with Doc, Joshua."

Joshua grinned, saying, "Shakespeare said, 'Life every man holds dear; but the brave man holds honor far more precious dear than life.' I feel the same toward you gentlemen. I consider you both new friends."

Doc tipped his hat brim, saying, "Yes, suh. He also said, 'In a false quarrel there is no true valor.' Let's hope that none of us have picked the wrong side to fight for."

Joshua grinned. "I am a Pinkerton. As the old saying goes, 'I ride for the brand.' I go where I am directed to go in my job. If we are pitted against each other, please understand I will still consider both of you with a great deal of respect and admiration."

Bat stuck out his hand, saying, "I think we are all of the same mind-set."

With that, the three men went their separate ways, each feeling good, yet uneasy about their concluding conversation.

Strongheart checked out and headed south through Lincoln Park toward his small spread south of Cañon City. As he climbed out of the emerald Arkansas River drainage, he started wondering what lay before him with Doc and Bat. Would they indeed fight each other, and if so, who would win?

Before him he could see the lesser peaks surrounding Cañon City, all under ten thousand feet. Well beyond was the giant Sangre de Cristo range like a western wall, which would block many storms without the courage to climb up over the thirteen- and fourteen-thousand-foot barrier. Those blizzards and storms that did make it over the top often would blow out over Cañon City and Florence and fall on the prairie out to the east.

Suddenly, Strongheart's hat flew sideways as he heard a crack as the first bullet flew past his head, and he immediately heard the thump sound from the muzzle blast, then a loud bang as a second shooter missed him. Both were in the trees, on two small hills surrounding Oak Creek Grade Stage Road, which climbed up over three thousand feet in elevation to the new mining town of Silver Cliff, a full day's or two days' ride southwest. He immediately swung down under Eagle's neck while the big paint bolted toward the trees to his right. Strongheart held on to the saddle with his left calf and wrapped his left arm around the horse's neck as he fired under the neck into the trees to his left. He heard more host right above him, but he knew the shooter to the right was firing blindly, as he heard bangs instead of that *crack-whump* sound when a bullet passes right by you. He swung up into the saddle, reloading while reining

Eagle with his knees. The paint instinctively knew Joshua was looking for that shooter. They came around a large clump of trees and there was a man, rifle in hand, trying to mount up on a big bay. Eagle slammed into the horse with his chest, sending him rolling sideways downhill on the backside of the small hill. The man hit the ground rolling and jumped up, shaking off the cobwebs.

He was a big man, Strongheart's height and solid, but his face was ugly and he looked like a giant rat with a narrow pointed nose and a tiny mouth that was pursed. Joshua almost grinned to himself, knowing this had to be Big Mouth Schwinn whom Doc Holliday had told him about, as the man had notches on the six-shooter on his hip. Joshua recognized it as a Colt Russian .44. The bushwhacker's right hand hovered over the holster as he wondered if he should draw.

Strongheart grinned. "Pull it. Bring that smokewagon out and go to work with it, and let's see what happens."

The shooter stood there, not knowing what to do.

Joshua said, "Your name is Schwinn?"

Schwinn said, "Yeah, how did you know?"

Strongheart said, "'Cause I heard they call you Big Mouth Schwinn, and I understand why. You are a curious-looking critter, Mister. Your mouth looks like the narrow end of a small funnel, and your face—well, you look just like a opossum."

The killer's face reddened as Strongheart said, "So,

before I go after your partner across the stage road, tell me, why did you varmints try to bushwhack me?"

"Yer a damned tin star Pinkerton and yer ridin' fer the Denver and Rio Grande in the railroad war, ain't ya?" Schwinn said.

"No," Strongheart replied. "Got that wrong. I might be tomorrow, but my boss hasn't given me marching orders yet. Why the notches on your gun? Fancy yourself a shooter?"

"I've kilt my share," the man said.

Joshua could tell from experience the man was working up the courage to draw. Strongheart didn't say a word, but just spun the pistol backward into his holster and smiled. Big Mouth's eyes widened suddenly, and Joshua drew with years of practice, seeing the man's pistol halfway out of his holster when the Pinkerton's pistol spit flame and a big red spot appeared in the middle of Schwinn's forehead and his body fell forward, dead and unmoving.

Strongheart now had to find the other bushwhacker quickly. He slowly rode Eagle back up the hill and moved from tree to tree, looking across at the other small piñon-covered hill, trying to spot the shooter. The man was not moving, and Joshua knew he had not taken off. Even though Joshua had been dealing with Big Mouth Schwinn, he had also automatically kept an eye on Eagle's ears, knowing the horse would warn him if the other bushwhacker tried to get out of the area or tried sneaking up behind him. The man was laying low.

Strongheart pulled his carbine out of the scabbard and cocked it. He aimed at the spot closest to where he thought the other ambusher was shooting from. He squeezed the trigger, and five seconds later the man took off at dead run from behind the hill on a big chestnut. Joshua put his front sight between the man's blades, then spurred Eagle into action while he stuck his carbine back into the scabbard. The black-and-white half-Arabian, half-saddlebred gelding started overtaking the big chestnut in short order. The killer galloped up Oak Creek Grade Stage Road, smacking his horse's withers with his long reins. Eagle was thrilled with the chase, and the more they angled uphill, the more ground he gained on the other horse.

When Strongheart was less than twenty feet behind him, the man whirled in his saddle, six-shooter in hand, and Joshua drew and fired. His fast point-and-pray technique worked, and the pistol flew out of the ambusher's hand as he screamed in pain. He spurred his horse even more, but Eagle was far superior, especially the farther they ran. The other heavily muscled horse was good for gathering cows and short bursts, but not longer distances, especially running uphill, which they had been doing within a half mile of the ambush spot. Arabian horses have larger nostrils, allowing them to take in more oxygen.

Joshua pulled up alongside the other man. He did not want him dead. He wanted to know how Schwinn knew who he was and where to lie in wait, and also why. He was certain that his meeting with Holliday and Masterson was simply coincidence. Nobody had gotten word to the two ambushers that fast. They had been waiting for him.

The horses were now side by side, and a large embankment ran off the west side of the road. Joshua jumped and slammed into the other man. They flew sideways, knocking the wind out of the shooter when he hit the ground and started rolling down the steep embankment. Joshua rolled, pushed with a foot and went into a shoulder roll, and then came up running. The man stood and staggered, and Strongheart slammed into him with a diving tackle. The shooter's eyes opened in panic, as he could not get his breath at all.

Strongheart jerked him up roughly and yelled, "Jump up and come down with your legs locked."

The panicked man jumped up in the air and came down on the ground with his knees locked and landed stiffly. The jolt jarred his wind back immediately and the panic feelings went away, but now he was being slapped across his face by a very powerful Joshua Strongheart. He tasted blood in his mouth, and blood spurted out of both nostrils.

His right hand bleeding with a bullet hole through it, he grabbed for his sheath knife with his left hand and desperately stabbed at Joshua. Strongheart sidestepped and the knife thrust went by his waist, and a vicious right fist arced and hit the man in the left cheekbone, shattering it. He hit the ground, and his left eye immediately started swelling shut. He was out.

When he awakened, he sputtered from the canteen water Joshua splashed on his face. The man was stout and wore all black clothes, had a black holster—basically, everything was black.

Strongheart stuck a prerolled cigarette in the man's mouth and lit it for him. He puffed long and deep, blowing out a blue tendril of smoke, which wafted away on the light mountain breeze.

Joshua said, "What's your name?"

The man said, "Stones Blackstone."

"Why were you and Big Mouth Schwinn trying to dry-gulch me?" Joshua asked. "That was Schwinn, wasn't it?"

Stones said through now-swollen lips, "Yes."

Joshua said, "Why did you two ambush me?"

Stones puffed thoughtfully and said, "Where is Big Mouth?"

Strongheart replied, "He has a new mouth in the middle of his forehead. I can arrange for you to have one, too, if you don't tell me what I want to know."

Blackstone said, "You outdrew Schwinn?"

Strongheart immediately replied, "No, I didn't. I had the drop on him and tied him up just like you are. He refused to answer my questions, so I shot him in the face."

Stones's eyes opened wider than when the wind was knocked out of him, and he started breathing very heavily.

He said, "What do you want to know?"

Joshua said, "I already asked you," and he cocked his gun.

Stones said, "He takes his orders from the big boss, V. R. Clinton. I ain't ever met him, but I know he told Big Mouth ta kill ya. Oncest we spotted you was in town, we set up at that spot, knowin' it was on the way ta yore spread. We been there since you and thet kid come ridin' inta town. I swear thet's all I know, sir. I swear it."

Strongheart said, "Why did he want me dead?"

Stones was almost in tears. "The only thing I heerd was thet you was on the side a the Denver and Rio Grande in the railroad war. Mr. Clinton wants you outta the way, cuz Big Mouth said you was a rattlesnake-mean hombre, especially when you drew iron. I seen myself he was right."

Strongheart led the man's horse over, picked Stones up, and placed him backward in his saddle. He lashed his bound wrists to the saddle horn. Stones panicked again.

Blackstone said, "What're ya doing? Ya ain't gonna hang me, are ya?"

Strongheart said, "I'm going to gag you if you don't shut up."

He checked his binding and mounted up on Eagle,

taking the man's reins in his hand, and headed back toward Cañon City. Stones was headed for the Fremont County Jail.

When they got to the ambush site, Strongheart dismounted, leaving Stones there behind on his horse. He walked Eagle around and found Big Mouth's horse, then took it to over to the body. He tied the man's body over his saddle, walked the gelding over behind Stones's horse, and tied the lead line around Stones's horse's tail and mounted up.

Joshua got many stares as he led his equine train down into Cañon City and to the sheriff's office. The sheriff greeted him when he rode up to the stone building on Macon Avenue. Scottie came riding up at a fast trot on his long-stepping Thoroughbred.

He jumped down and ran over to his hero, saying excitedly, "What happened, Joshua?"

It wasn't the first time he had called his mentor by his first name, but he still felt funny doing so, though it also made him feel more grown-up. After all, Strongheart had insisted he call him that.

Strongheart, grinning, said, "Well, I saw this feller riding his horse backward pulling the other one, so I thought I should lead them back to Cañon City and introduce them to the sheriff here."

The sheriff and the young lad both chuckled.

Joshua said, "Come on, Scottie. You can listen in while I tell the sheriff all about it, if he has some coffee made."

The sheriff said, "No, but I'll send a deputy for some good coffee from the café. You want some milk, Scottie?"

"No, sir," Scottie replied, puffing his chest out. "I'd like some coffee, too, Sheriff. Thank you, sir."

Grinning, the lawman and Strongheart gave each other a knowing look as they thought back to their own emergent teenaged years.

Over coffee, Joshua told them both the story, beginning with his meeting with Doc Holliday and Bat Masterson. He also told the sheriff about V. R. Clinton and wondered what he knew about him.

The sheriff said, "Loner. Total loner. He has a big, big house up in the Wet Mountain Valley, and we have not been able to find out anything about him, except he is surrounded by gun toughs and nobody but a few of them ever sees him. This Percival Schwinn you killed was one of his shootists, but the man acted like a dude. He even had notches carved in his gun."

Strongheart laughed out loud, interrupting. "Percival? Did you say Percival? No wonder he had a nickname."

The sheriff laughed and slapped his right thigh.

He went on. "Maybe we can find out more, since you brought this Stones back alive. We do not know where his money came from, but he has bought up large parcels of land between Cotopaxi and Pueblo and just sits on it."

"Mighty interesting," Strongheart said. "Wonder if we have any info on him? I'll find out. I have to go send a telegraph about the shooting anyway. Come on, Scottie."

The two rode to the Western Union office and Strongheart explained as he wrote, "When you send a telegraph, you say as much as you can with as few words as possible."

The telegrapher said, "Mr. Strongheart, we have a telegram here for you. Came several days ago from Chicago. So much excitement with our break-in the other day, and I heard you weren't in town."

Joshua said, "Break-in?"

The telegrapher said, "Yep. Didn't steal anything, but broke in through a side window. Telegrapher was out delivering an important telegram to a rancher way up in the north end of town, toward Red Canyon. They did steal three dollars, but that was all that was here, except for the hidden safe."

Strongheart read his telegram and saw it was from his boss, Lucky. "Investigate railroad war STOP We are on side of D and RG STOP Good luck STOP."

That answered his question about how Big Mouth Schwinn or his boss found out Strongheart was on the side of the Denver and Rio Grande.

He wrote a quick report about the shooting and then added, "Need info on V. R. Clinton wealthy rancher south of Westcliffe STOP."

Now Strongheart knew where he was standing with the railroad war, but his first thought was he hoped he would not have to have a shootout with Doc Holliday and Bat Masterson. Besides them, Joshua knew they had a gang of seventy gun toughs, including the infamous Ben Thompson and Dirty Dave Rudabaugh. The latter had earned that nickname not because of his ruthless gunplay, but because of his bathing and personal hygiene habits. In short, Dirty Dave Rudabaugh was, well, usually dirty and smelly.

Joshua remained at the Western Union office, which was at the railroad depot, while he and Lucky exchanged messages. Then Joshua and Scottie left there, riding west.

8

PUEBLO?

At First Street, Strongheart stopped and instructed Scottie, "Pack your saddlebags and bedroll and tell your aunt. Tomorrow morning, we'll leave for Pueblo for several days. Make sure it is okay with her."

"Okay, Joshua, but I know it will be," Scottie said enthusiastically, and he rode off with a wave.

Strongheart turned right and rode to Main Street, just a block away, and turned east. He walked Eagle slowly through town, not realizing that many of the people looking at him thought about the fact that they were looking at a living legend. Strongheart was unaware that some men resented him and were jealous, and that many women looked at him and thought that if only their husband possessed this good trait or that good trait of Strongheart's, all would be better with her world. Many women also simply looked at him and pictured in their mind's eye what it would be like making love with the tall, well-muscled, handsome romantic.

He had planned to do a little shopping for some supplies and foodstuffs. It was much easier to ride the train between Pueblo and Cañon City and did not take that long, but Joshua wanted to make the forty-one-mile ride and poke around a little bit at some of the parcels of land that Clinton owned. Lucky did not have any immediate information or intelligence on the wealthy landowner, but pledged to check him out as much as possible.

He shopped for some supplies and would eat in town. There was a new place simply called the French Restaurant that he wanted to try out, as he had heard some good comments about it. Because of the hot mineral springs and favorable climate, Cañon City was becoming a tourist town, so there always seemed to be a few nice restaurants around.

Strongheart walked into the small café right at dark and saw candles everywhere, melted into the tops of empty French wine bottles.

An attractive waitress walked up to him and said, "*Bonsoir, monsieur.* Welcome. Where would you like to sit?"

Strongheart pointed at a corner table and said, "*Bonsoir, mademoiselle. Comment allez-vous?*"

She looked surprised and smiled flirtatiously, flicking

her long eyelashes as she replied, *"Je vais bien, merci, monsieur. Et vous?"*

Strongheart smiled, saying, *"Bien, merci,"* as he sat down in the corner facing the door, as always.

She handed him the menu, and he started looking at items and was impressed.

"A wine, *monsieur*?" she asked.

"Non, merci, but I am ready to order. I'll have *bœuf l'entrecôte à la Provençal et sa ratatouille, s'il vous plaît?"*

"Mais oui, monsieur! Très bien," she said. "An excellent selection."

He said, "How did Cañon City get a fine French restaurant like this?"

Just then the door opened, and a ravishingly beautiful woman walked in. Her hair was not just blond but looked like sunlight with melting honey dripping off of it, and it was naturally curly, yet hung all the way down her very slim waistline. Above that were a very shapely and firm bust and one of the most classically beautiful faces Joshua had ever seen.

She smiled at the waitress, saying, *"Bonsoir,* Michelle. Sir, the owner of the restaurant was a very successful chef in Paris, but was bound and determined to move to America, travel to the frontier, and pan and mine for gold. After leaving many holes in the ground, he decided to return to France, but was almost broke. He discovered this was a tourist area because of the wonderful climate here, the fishing, and the medicinal hot springs nearby, *et voilà*! The French Restaurant was born. Do you want company for dinner?"

He stood and held her chair for her with a smile and a nod, saying, "With such beauty, nothing could go better with fine food and this atmosphere. My name is Joshua Strongheart."

She said, "Helena Victoria. Please to meet you, sir. Would you like to order for me? I like everything."

Joshua smiled, saying, "You are easy to please."

She quickly replied, "I have very high standards, but am easy to please once they are met."

He said, "Well, with such beauty you should. And you even have a very beautiful name to go with your looks."

"Thank you," she said demurely.

Strongheart said to the waitress, "A white wine for the lady, please, and I will order for her."

Michelle said, "*Oui, monsieur.* And I need to know how you want your steak cooked?"

"Medium rare. And bring me coffee, please?" he responded. "The lady would like *coquilles St. Jacques à la Provençal et sa riz de veau et sa ratatouille*."

"*Oui, monsieur, merci.*"

She brought a glass of white wine for Helena, who nodded her appreciation, and Strongheart found himself lost in her bright green eyes. He had never seen such a striking color of eyes in his life.

She said, "Your French is excellent, and you are

eating here and not in a saloon down the street, and the way you are dressed . . . Frankly, are you an Indian or a cowboy or a world traveler?"

Strongheart laughed. "I am a Pinkerton agent."

"A Pinkerton agent who speaks French?" She laughed. "That one caught me off guard. I would not have guessed."

Strongheart grinned. "My father was a Lakota warrior. My mother was white. She was a teenaged girl traveling West with a wagon train, but her parents were both tragically killed en route. She was left by the wagon train in Montana Territory."

"My word!" said Helena.

Joshua continued, "Her parents were going to open a mercantile store, and she was left in the middle of the wilderness with two large Conestoga wagons filled with goods, then was attacked by a large grizzly bear. My father was a Lakota—you call us Sioux—warrior and he happened upon her and fought the grizzly, getting mauled horribly, but he killed it. She nursed him back to health out there in a lonely mountain valley. Nine months later, I was born, and he rode off with a wave."

"What a story!" she said. "How fascinating! Then what happened to your mother?"

Joshua said, "I did not mean to get into such detail and dominate the conversation."

"Nonsense," she said. "I am enthralled with the story, sir. Please tell me?"

"Well," he said, "please call me Joshua, not sir. They

were there a little while and she knew she was in the family way. So, my father told her that they could not go anywhere and love as a couple. Their worlds were too different."

"Heavens to Betsy!" she said. "Then what happened?"

"Sadly, he gave her this knife and sheath"—and Joshua pulled them off his gun belt and sat them before her—"and told her he knew they would have a son. He said he would tell his family and tribe about her, so she could travel there freely with me and I could be taught his ways. I was also to be given this knife when old enough and was to keep it very sharp and clean. Then, he hugged her, hopped on his pony, and rode off into the mountains. She never got over him."

"Oh," Helena said, and dabbed at her eyes with a hanky, and then admired the knife.

Strongheart said, "My mother opened a mercantile in a small town, where I was born. She fell in love with a tall, quiet lawman named Dan Trooper and married him. He became my father and was very strict, but I knew he loved me. He taught me to shoot and fight. My mother made a lot of money and inherited a lot, too. She made sure I got an education. That was very important to her."

"Oh my," she said. "Where did you matriculate?"

"Princeton," Joshua said.

"Princeton!" she said. "Did you graduate?"

Strongheart said, "Yes, I got my baccalaureate degree."

"What did you major in?"

He grinned. "Philosophy, with a minor in English literature."

"You just get more and more fascinating!" she cooed.

Strongheart said, "Well, it must be your eyes, but that is the most I have ever spoken about myself, and it is enough. More than enough."

Their meals were brought out and served and both thought them to be very delicious.

He finished a mouthful of wonderful steak, saying afterward, "Did you get an education?"

"Oh yes," she said. "I grew up back East, a very proper young lady. I went to a series of private girls' schools and graduated from Wesleyan College in Macon, Georgia, suh," she said, inflecting her speech with a Southern accent and a chuckle.

"It was the first women's college in the nation. Now, just in the past few years, they have been opening more colleges for women," she said. "I majored in business."

"What brought you out West?" Strongheart asked.

"Adventure," she said with a smile revealing thirty-two perfect white teeth.

This woman was taking Joshua's breath away.

"How is your food?" he said.

"It is delicious," she replied. "Here, have a bite."

She held a forkful of food up, and Strongheart gobbled it down.

He said, "I hope this restaurant stays in business.

This food is very good. This is a restaurant I would expect to see in Chicago, or maybe Denver."

He thought about her offering him the bite of her meal. That was very forward and unusual in that day and time. He knew she was teasing him, but he did not mind one bit. He briefly thought about Brenna Alexander, whom he had been seeing some when in Chicago and who he knew was serious about him. Then he wondered why he even thought anything about it. They were not betrothed. As always, although he forbid himself from thinking about it, he also envisioned his first cousin, Wiya Waste (Wee-ya Waas-Tay), whose name meant "beautiful woman." She had always been madly in love with Joshua and had offered herself to him, but he would not let himself fall prey to her tremendous beauty and charm, because they were cousins. He still could never think about any pretty woman, though, without first thinking of her. He was very proud that she was family, because she had such quality to her.

Helena spoke about fine restaurants in various cities, but Strongheart had to concentrate on the three men who walked in and took seats at a table nearby. They did not fit in this restaurant. These three were hard cases. One was an Apache-turned-cowboy-gunfighter, one was Mexican, and the third was white and possessed a pair of the most evil eyes Strongheart had ever seen. They were almost slits, and with his angular jawline, the man reminded Joshua clearly of a rattlesnake. Strongheart's mind was cataloguing potential threats while politely listening to the beauty across from him. The rattler face wore twin cross-draw Colt .45s, but he had a suit jacket on with a bulge under his left armpit, so he had a hideout gun there, too. The Mexican did not realize it, but when he moved, Joshua could make out the outline of the knife he had sheathed down the back of his shirt, between the shoulder blades. Strongheart sensed that knife could be thrown and strike any target in the room accurately and swiftly. He also wore a .44 on his left. Strongheart could tell it had not been drawn over and over by the lack of wear and tear on the leather rough-out holster. The Apache would be his biggest threat, because like Strongheart, he wore a Colt .45 Peacemaker on his right hip and a long Bowie-sized knife on his left hip. Joshua saw that both the sheath and the holster had worn spots where this man had drawn both weapons in practice over and over. His face was expressionless, and this lack of emotion really put Joshua on the alert. These three were up to no good. He could sense it. The warrior's sense.

This woman sent stirrings in Joshua that made him feel very unsettled. That feeling he did not like. He was trying to be cordial, even flirty with her, but at the same time, he knew these shooters were indeed here for him, just waiting.

After their meal, they both drank some delicious coffee while making small talk. He could even tell that the three men made the waitress uncomfortable.

He had to act and act fast. They were shifting,

unsettled themselves, and even moved their chairs so they could draw pistols if needed in the French Restaurant. The men were getting antsy and wanted to kill.

Strongheart stood and said, "Helena, excuse me. I just remembered, I did not unsaddle my horse, and he's been wearing it too long. I will be right back, okay?"

She smiled pleasantly and nodded, but hated being left alone with the three men at the nearby table, who looked like miscreants. After Strongheart left, the Apache got up from the table and followed him outside. The livery stable was next door, so he slipped into the shadows, drawing his pistol, and followed where he figured Joshua had gone. He moved silently through the shadows and worked his way along the wall by one of the two big open doors and into the doorway of the large stable. A lasso dropped down from the hayloft above and fell to the ground around his ankles. It was quickly pulled tight, and the gunman was jerked upward by the force of Strongheart holding the other end of the rope, which passed over a pulley, and Strongheart went to the ground while looking up at the Apache, grinning. Joshua held up the Apache's knife. He had grabbed it as he passed the man going upward, ripping it out of the Apache's sheath. His gun had also fallen out of his holster and was lying on the ground at Strongheart's feet. The Apache, seeing the knife, automatically reached for the pistol, then the knife, even though he could see it in Strongheart's hand. Joshua tied the rope to a nearby corral post.

The Apache seethed and said through gritted teeth, "When I get down, you will die, Lakota pig!"

Strongheart pulled out his giant knife and held the scalpel-sharp blade above the rope, saying, "Fine, I will let you down very fast so you can do that."

The Apache's eyes opened wide in panic as he looked down at the ground twenty-some feet below him.

Joshua held the knife against the rope and said, "Quickly, who sent you three to kill me?"

The Apache did not deny it. He glared at Joshua and did not speak. Joshua sawed a few strands of the rope away.

He said, "Wonder how much cutting this rope can take before it snaps?"

The Apache said, "Wait! Stop! I will tell you. It was our boss, V. R. Clinton."

"Why?" Joshua said.

The Apache replied, "I do not know. Honest. I do not know. I get paid much money and do what the foreman says. I think they do not want you to fight for the Denver and Rio Grande."

The Pinkerton said, "The foreman, his name?"

The Apache replied, "You killed him. One top hand speaks like foreman now. His name is Fast Norm Megilligan."

Strongheart sheathed his knife and walked over to the blacksmith's fire, which still had some glowing embers in it. He pulled out two bullets from his gun and dropped them in the coals, grabbed another rope off the wall, and returned to the restaurant. He quickly tied the rope off across the doorway at ankle height, stepped over it, and walked through the door.

Smiling at Helena, he said, "I am very sorry. I had to take care of the horse. You now will have my undivided attention."

She smiled and he listened. The two henchmen whispered and apparently were wondering where their partner was. Then the two bullets went off, one after the other. Both men grabbed their pistols and ran out the door.

Joshua stood and said to Helena, "Stay here and move away from the door!"

Her eyes opened wide, but she listened and moved toward the kitchen as he bolted out the door.

Outside, the two men were sprawled in the dirt and were spinning around, clawing for their pistols. Strongheart drew and fired. He hit the one on the left in the chest with his first bullet, fanned the hammer back with his left hand, and shot the other in the stomach, then immediately followed that with a second bullet that slammed into his chest. The one on the left brought his gun up, but Strongheart fanned another shot into his chest a few inches from the first one. The one on the right looked dead, but the one on the left sure was game. He tried to stand but only got up on one knee, bubbles coming out of one bullet hole, and he slowly raised his pistol again. Joshua fired again, but the gun went *click*, and he did a border shift, tossing the Peacemaker into his left hand as his right hand went to his knife sheath, pulled the large knife out, and flipped it over, and his hand went forward, the blade slipping through his fingers. The knife spun over a half a spin and buried itself up to the hilt in the killer's chest. This blade went through his heart, killing him instantly. He fell forward on his face. Strongheart quickly thumbed shells into his pistol, cursing himself for not replacing bullets when he tossed the two rounds into the fire. While he checked the two men to ensure the danger was gone, he once again thought back to his expensive lesson with his father growing up.

The tall Pinkerton agent went into the restaurant and saw that Helena was visibly shaken. A crowd was forming outside, and a sheriff's deputy came in the door, gun drawn. Strongheart was holding Helena, who was trembling. She put her head on his shoulder and whimpered a little.

Strongheart said, "I killed those two outside. Their partner, a gun hand who looks to be a Mescalero Apache, is hanging upside down from a rope at the livery stable."

He looked down at Helena's beautiful face and grinned, saying, "I fibbed. I did not want to alarm you, but I could tell those three were after me. I tricked the Apache into following me, and I lassoed him and hung him upside down. He's still alive."

Helena said, "I want to see him, please."

He took her outside and thought about how different this beauty was from Annabelle, his late fiancée, and

Beautiful Woman, his first cousin. Neither of them would have been frightened like Helena was.

Two deputies were with the men Joshua killed, and he and Helena went on to the livery stable. The deputy who had run into the restaurant was there, and he turned and looked grimly at Strongheart.

He was clearly upset and said, "Mr. Strongheart, I have all the respect in the world for you, but I always heerd you was one ta ride the river with and would always fight fair and square. I got ta ask, sir, why would ya slit this Apache's throat when he is upside down and ain't heeled?"

Strongheart moved forward, exclaiming, "What?"

He looked at the Apache, who was now hanging lifeless upside down with a giant pool of fresh blood under him.

He said, "Deputy, I didn't kill him. I hung him here upside down, but I left him a few minutes ago. Please keep people back and check for tracks. Somebody, who has to still be close, came in right behind me, and slit his throat."

The deputy looked down at the ground, and said to a man standing close, "Run into the café and see if they have a lantern. Hurry!"

A minute later, the man emerged with a large lantern, which was throwing a lot of light. The deputy used it, and sure enough found boot prints of a heavy man with large feet who had approached from behind the stable and run off pretty much in the same direction. He followed the tracks for a while, but they went into the side street, where he lost them in the other tracks. He was still in town, maybe even in the large group of watchers assembling.

He returned to the body and said, "You were right, Mr. Strongheart. There was a killer, and he is still in town, a big, heavy man with large boots. Sorry for accusing you."

Strongheart chuckled. "You are doing your job and do not apologize. Just call me Joshua, please, or Strongheart, just not *Mister*. At least you're a man who is not afraid to speak his mind."

He could see the deputy's chest puff out a little and his chin lift up with pride.

The deputy said, "Let me interview this lady, sir. Then I'll speak with you fully. Boys, keep people away from the bodies!"

Joshua walked into the café, got a cup of coffee, and went back out, sitting down on a stump near the stable and thinking back to his father and his stern upbringing. It was a story he had relived in his mind many times.

Joshua longed for a father, and he was excited as a young man when the town marshal of the blossoming community of Flower Valley, Dan Trooper, got serious about his ma. Marshal Trooper was tall and slender, maybe six-foot-two and 190 pounds, but that was all muscle and sinew from all the years of hard work.

The marshal had high cheekbones, a prominent nose, and honest, intelligent hazel eyes which would bore daggers through anybody. Much older than Joshua's ma, he had a little gray in his mustache, which was always well trimmed and ran full down in a point just past the corner of each thin lip. Like his hair, it was primarily dark brown.

He was not given to talking, just doing. Dan was a very harsh taskmaster to Joshua when he was growing up, but he was all man, and he was bound and determined to make his stepson a man. He said the country was too unforgiving for him to go easy on the boy.

The man was great with grappling and fistfighting much larger men, spending many hours tossing around a large section of heavy log with thick branches simulating arms and legs. He made Joshua train and build his muscles with it, too.

Dan was also an incredible shot with rifle or pistol. He started Joshua when he was young and first taught him how to shoot a long gun. He had learned to shoot with an 1860 Henry .44 repeater, and his stepdad gave it to him when he was twelve years old.

It caused Joshua to chuckle because he realized he was rubbing his fanny while he looked across at Helena being interviewed. He thought about the lesson his father had taught him about keeping track of his ammunition, and he could not believe he had not reloaded after tossing the two bullets into the blacksmith's fire.

It was another hour before Strongheart and Helena

were able to leave. He walked her down Main Street and could tell she was still unnerved by the situation. They arrived at her hotel, and she turned at the doorway outside.

Looking up into his dark eyes, she said, "Mr. Strongheart, Joshua, I can tell you are a true gentleman, part Indian or not. I am still shaking from what happened."

Inside, Joshua shivered when she said "part Indian or not," and it bothered him. He decided it was too trivial to concern himself about. His entire life, he had grown up hearing "half-breed" derisively, "blanket nigger," "red nigger," "Injun," "redskin," "mongrel," and "cur," and many of his white friends called him "Chief." Strongheart chalked it all up to ignorance.

"I know this is very, very forward, Joshua," she said. "We just met, but I really do not want to be alone tonight. Would you please escort me to my room and stay with me tonight and just hold me?"

Strongheart got a lump in his throat. This was not only one of the most beautiful women he had ever seen, but one of, if not the most, sensuous woman he had ever laid his eyes on.

Always the gentleman, the tall half-breed simply said, "Of course."

They went upstairs to her room, which was the top suite in the hotel. Inside the room, she immediately turned and moved into his arms. They came together in a long, lingering kiss.

Stepping back, she whispered, "Hold me, please?"

Strongheart wrapped his massive, muscular arms around her, and she laid her head on his chest, her breathing shallow. Something about this made him uncomfortable. Maybe he still felt a loyalty to his late fiancée, but he did not think so. He would always love Belle and always mourn her, but he had emotionally processed her death. He was romantically involved with Brenna Alexander. He even had fantasies about his ravishing Sioux cousin Beautiful Woman, who was so aptly named. There was just something about this, maybe because they had just met or because she was being the aggressor. Something inside just felt awkward.

She asked him to have a seat in the sitting room while she slipped into something more comfortable. She emerged minutes later in a pink silk gown covering a matching sheer outfit. Joshua knew this woman had money.

She sat down and said, "Joshua, would you like a nightcap or coffee?"

He said, "What are you having?"

She said, "I am going to order a small glass of brandy."

He said, "I will have an iced tea if they have it."

She smiled and pulled a long cord in the ceiling. A bell rang downstairs, and in minutes a young bellman knocked on her door.

She said, "Can you bring me a small brandy and a glass of tea, iced tea, from the saloon downstairs, please?"

He tipped his cap and took off running.

The pair made small talk until the bellboy returned with the drinks. She tipped him handsomely, and he left, very excited.

Strongheart said, "Thank you, Helena. I do not drink liquor, but I discovered iced tea, a brand-new drink, several years ago and like it. Do you want to try a sip?"

He held his glass out to her. She smiled softly, putting her hand up.

Helena said, "Thank you, no. I have had iced tea and do enjoy it occasionally."

Because Strongheart had that uncomfortable feeling, and simply because he was a warrior and an investigator, he noticed everything and made mental notes constantly. She sipped her brandy and held the glass out for a toast, and they touched glasses and he sipped his tea.

She said, "Can you do me a favor and get that suitcase for me and set it on the bed? It is very heavy."

"Certainly," he said, feeling tipsy when he stood up.

He picked up the suitcase by the dresser and set it on the bed, noticing it really was not that heavy. When he turned, Helena was standing in front of her chair, her gown and robe on the floor. She was totally nude, and her naked body was even more perfect than he had imagined. It was flawless, in fact. He got very dizzy and had to grab the bedpost to steady himself.

She said, "I must confess, I didn't really want you to just hold me tonight. I wanted you to love me."

He started getting dizzier and suddenly realized that she had put something in his drink. The look on her face turned from seductive to evil, and his mind raced and whirled. He staggered to the window and remembered there was an awning over the first-floor windows below, and he shook his head to clear the cobwebs. He was confused, but his survival instincts as a warrior took over. Joshua saw her reaching for something in her purse and thought he saw the handle of a Bulldog pistol, and he staggered across the room and crashed headfirst through the window. He fell three stories and was able to make himself twist so his body hit the awning with his back muscles. He heard her startled scream behind and then above him.

He immediately rolled off the awning, hitting the ground below with a thump, bruising his hip and upper arm. Strongheart knew he was in danger, and his eyes slowly scanned the scene. He moved along the building, leaning against it for support, and went around the corner to the back side, where she could not see his movements. Spotting a wooden building with a raised wooden side-walk, he made his way across the street and dived head-first under the wooden walkway. Strongheart crawled as fast as he could under the building, hearing rodents scatter left and right. In total darkness, he curled into a fetal position and passed out amid the sounds of men running around yelling to each other, looking for him.

Strongheart opened his eyes, and his head swirled. He was in darkness and heard something moving. He wondered if he was in a teepee in his father's family circle. His head hurt and his eyes closed.

Beautiful Woman, his cousin, came into the teepee and told him, "Do not worry. I will watch over you, Wanji Wambli." She removed her antelope-skin dress and it fell around her ankles. Her beauty was breathtaking, and he opened his arms. She fell into them, and their lips came together. She reached down and grabbed his wrist, pulling on it, and he came wide awake with a start.

"Don't shoot!" Scottie's voice quietly but emphatically said in the darkness.

Joshua blinked his eyes and realized he had drawn his gun and Scottie Middleton was holding his wrist.

Scottie let go and whispered, "Joshua, it is me, Scottie. Something happened to you and men are looking for you. You can sleep. I will watch out for you."

Strongheart smiled in the blackness under the building, and his eyes closed again. He wished he could go back to his dream with his cousin in it.

It was full daylight out in the street when Strongheart opened his eyes and started blinking them. Scottie Middleton lay between him and the street outside and had his head resting on his left hand, his pistol in his right hand. Joshua grinned.

"Are they gone?" he whispered.

Scottie jumped with a start.

He said, "Yes, sir. I think it is safe to crawl out now."

They both crawled out into the sunlight and stood up. A few onlookers on the street looked shocked. Strongheart felt woozy and shook his head to clear the dizzy feeling. His head felt like a blacksmith was within his skull using the inside of his temples for an anvil while pounding away on mental horseshoes. His entire body felt like he had fallen down a cliff, a very high cliff, banging against rocks all the way down.

Joshua walked over to a nearby watering trough, stepped in between two horses, and shoved his head down into the cold water. He pulled it out, shaking it vigorously, his long black ponytail whipping from side to side like a teamster cracking a bullwhip. The water really did help him awaken a little, and he turned to Scottie and stuck out his hand. They shook, and the boy's shoulders went back. Strongheart knew this boy had saved his life, but he wanted his head to clear up before they spoke about what had happened.

Joshua drew his Peacemaker to check the weapon for dirt, damages, and bullets. It was okay. He did so while walking fast with large strides. Scottie almost had to run to keep up with him.

Strongheart strode into the hotel lobby and up to the front desk. The manager recognized him, but had no idea about what had happened the night before; just that a window had gotten broken in the luxury suite.

Joshua said, "Did Helena Victoria check out yet?"

The man said, "Helena Victoria, what a beautiful name. I would recognize such a name, sir, but will check the register."

He looked and said, "No, sir. Nobody by that name has registered here."

Strongheart said, "There was a beautiful lady with very long, blond hair who was in the executive suite last night. Is she still here, and what name did she register under?"

The manager said, "I definitely know who you mean, Mr. Strongheart. Quite a good-looking filly, I must say. But, sir, you know I cannot divulge such information."

Joshua said, "Of course," and tossed five dollars down on the counter.

Without saying a word, the man scooped the money into his pocket and produced the register. Turning it toward Strongheart, he tapped the name with his index finger. It read: "Helen Smith." It also indicated that she had checked out at 4:30 A.M.

Strongheart hissed under his breath. Nodding, he turned, with Scottie following him as he headed toward the French Restaurant. Just as he and Scottie walked up to the establishment, the waitress who had served him the night before walked out the front door, locking it behind her.

She turned and smiled seeing the tall, dark, handsome man again.

"Bonjour monsieur, comment allez-vous?"

He doffed his hat, saying, *"Bonjour, mademoiselle, je vais bien. Merci. Et vous?"*

She replied, *"Je vais bien,"* then explained, "The owner, the chef, ees my fiancé. We are closed for breakfast, but lunch is *très bien.*"

143

Strongheart said, "No, I just wondered if you saw the young lady I met here last night with the shooting?"

She said, "No, *monsieur.*"

Strongheart said, "Does she come often?"

She said, "Only zees past week. She came several times to eat and said she loved our food."

Joshua said, "What name did she use?"

"Helena Victoria, *monsieur*, a beautiful name to be sure," she replied.

"Yes, it is," Joshua said. "Did she say where she was from?"

"*Oui, monsieur*, Santa Fe, but she said she sometimes stays in Pueblo."

Strongheart said, "Did she say anything else of any interest, or anything unusual?"

"*Non,*" she replied. "What ees eet you Americans say? Ah, just small talk."

He said, "Thank you very much. You've been very helpful. *Au revoir.*"

"You are welcome, *monsieur.* Good morning," she said, as he stepped aside to let her walk toward downtown.

"Come on," Strongheart said. "Let's go see the sheriff, then we have to wire my boss."

Five minutes later, they were sitting in the sheriff's office on Macon Street and briefed the sheriff on what had happened. Joshua learned that Scottie came out in the middle of the night ready to go with Joshua and too excited to sleep. From two blocks away, he saw Joshua crash out the window and make his way to the building across the street. Almost immediately, obvious gun toughs were out looking for him. Scottie hid among the shadows and finally crawled under the building, where he sat watch over Strongheart for hours. The Pinkerton was very impressed.

When they finished, the sheriff said to Scottie, "You did a fine and brave thing, young man, but we need to get you to school."

Strongheart said, "School? I thought you were out of school right now. Why didn't you tell me?"

Scottie grinned, saying, "You didn't ask, Joshua. Besides, I want to help you solve this case. I think I can."

Strongheart said, "If you want to be a good Pinkerton, or just a good man, you need to get your education. Thank you very much, Scottie, for what you did, but off to school. We'll leave when you're out."

Scottie shuffled toward the door and said, "Yes, sir. I have two more days, then vacation."

Strongheart and the sheriff looked at each other and chuckled.

"What now?" the sheriff asked.

Joshua said, "I'll send a telegraph to Lucky and head to Westcliffe. You said this V. R. Clinton has a ranch south of Westcliffe. I need a map of it and the area around it, Sheriff."

The sheriff said, "Have one right here with his ranch marked. Don't get yourself shot."

Strongheart grinned and headed toward the door. Minutes later, he rode up to the Western Union office and sent a telegraph to Lucky. He stuck around and a half hour later got a response. Lucky had written: "Still no intel on V. R. Clinton STOP Be careful STOP."

9

WESTCLIFFE

Strongheart headed up South Ninth Street on his way to Silver Cliff and then nearby Westcliffe. He would arrive the next day, after camping overnight in the Greenhorn Mountains.

Joshua rode up to a small café in the fairly new town of Westcliffe shortly after sunrise. He saw a buckboard loaded with mercantile goods outside and a team of four mules hooked up to it, and he felt it looked familiar. Walking in the door, he saw the grinning face of his friend Zachariah Banta from Cotopaxi, who motioned him over.

Strongheart sat down after shaking hands with Zach. The white-haired, white-bearded old-timer said,

"Wal, I reckon yore breakfast will be here in a few minutes. Here comes yer coffee now."

A waitress walked up with a cup of steaming hot coffee.

Joshua grinned at Zach and said to the waitress, "Is it strong?"

Zach interrupted before she could answer. "Wal, I reckon it is. She brung me my cup, and I asked her the same durned question. So, I simply walked outside. Did you see them purty rosebushes they have?"

Joshua, laughing, nodded.

Zach went on. "Wal, I grabbed me three a them big white rocks they had round them rosebushes. I brung 'em in here and dropped 'em in mah cup. All three of them plopped intah the coffee, then floated back up the surface. They jest floated around on top of thet coffee, like three little swans in a dirty pond."

Strongheart and the waitress both laughed heartily, and she returned to the kitchen.

Joshua said, "Thanks for having her bring me coffee, Zach, but how'd you know my breakfast is coming? I haven't even looked at the menu."

Zach said, "Wal, I reckon, young man, I got a brain in mah noggin. I was lookin' at the window over theah, and seen me a tall Injun, or mebbe a cowboy, who was riding thet big ole beautiful black-and-white fancy dancer horse, so I ordered ya four eggs, a big steak, rare, taters, and biscuits, and afterward, a fresh piece a home-made apple pie. Am Ah a good boy?"

Strongheart nodded. "Yes, you are a good boy. Thank you."

Joshua found out that Zach had been in Pueblo, fifty-five miles due east and four thousand feet lower in elevation than Westcliffe, buying supplies. He had business in Westcliffe, so he climbed up to the eight-thousand-foot-high valley, and would then go north a day's ride to Cotopaxi. It would have been easier to drive his wagon from Pueblo to Cañon City and then along the river to Cotopaxi, but it was actually a much shorter route going through Westcliffe.

Strongheart's food came, and he dug in, while Zach ate a similar meal.

Then, gulping some coffee, he said, "Old-timer, I have a mystery to solve, and you seem to know everyone from here to there and everything that happens."

Banta grinned.

Joshua swallowed a bite of steak and said, "V. R. Clinton lives south of here, on a big spread, and I know he hired guns for the Atchison, Topeka and Santa Fe in this railroad war that is going on. I don't know why, but he seems to have plenty of money. What is his stake in this railroad war? Why doesn't anybody know him or anything about him?"

Zach said, "Joshua, I am stumped mahself. I have heered all about this old boy, but cain't find nothin' out about him or his business."

Strongheart said, "I'm going to sneak onto his place and see what I can learn. What I do not understand is why he wants to back the Atchison, Topeka and Santa Fe in this railroad war. If I could figure out that tie-in, maybe then I can solve what's going on.

"What can you tell me about the history of Westcliffe and this area? Maybe there is a clue there why he moved here and what he has up his sleeve," Joshua said. "Also, why has he sent gun toughs after me? Night before last, I met a beautiful woman who lured me to her hotel room in Cañon City and then slipped a Mickey into my iced tea. I managed to escape and hide, but there were gun toughs looking for me all night. That young Scottie Middleton happened to see me hide, and he put the sneak on all of them and kept watch over me until I came to yesterday."

Zach said, "I been keepin' tabs on thet boy, and he is sumtin. Shore taken a shine to you. Wal, if ya want ta know the history of this area, we better order more coffee."

Zach then went into detail, telling Strongheart the history of the whole Wet Mountain Valley area.

Custer County was one of the most beautiful, pristine spots in the world and was teeming with elk, antelope, bison, mule deer, bears, wolves, and fish, and although it was at eight thousand feet elevation, the valley had lots of natural irrigation, sunshine, moisture, and good soil. It was ideal for growing crops and grazing cattle. It began as a favorite gathering place for many American Indians, a tradition that lasted for centuries. Then in the mid–

fifteen hundreds, the Spanish conquistadors arrived, hoping to annex the lands, find gold and silver, trade with the Indians, and convert the Indians to Christianity so they would be allies and not enemies. After that were the explorers: Lieutenant Zebulon Pike, Lieutenant John C. Fremont, and famed frontier scout Kit Carson, all in the early eighteen hundreds. Like they had done all over the West, adventurous mountain men and fur trappers followed the explorers. Some of them stayed in the Wet Mountain Valley and surrounding mountain ranges to trap beaver, hunt bison, elk, deer, and other game, and build trading posts.

Then, around 1869, the first settlers and pioneers arrived. Elisha P. Horn, John Taylor, and William Vorhis were three of the more powerful ones, and each claimed a section of the valley. Elisha Horn settled near the base of one large fourteen-thousand-plus-foot peak, which was named Horn's Peak after him. Taylor placed his spread on what was named Taylor Creek, and Vorhis helped found the town of Dora.

A year later, German colonists journeyed to the valley after leaving Chicago. Their leader was Carl Wulsten, and another of the prominent fourteeners was named after him, Wulsten's Baldy Peak. They left Chicago by train and traveled as far as they could, then got Conestoga wagons from Fort Lyons, far to the east of Pueblo out on the prairie. They started a new town fifteen miles west of where Westcliffe would be located and named the new town Colfax, after the then-current Vice President Schuyler Colfax.

In less than a year the town failed because of the lack of experience and knowledge about farming and ranching. The original one hundred families disappeared from Wet Mountain Valley; however, a few, such as Carl Wulsten, remained and claimed individual plots of land under the Homestead Act. He worked and found success, in fact, as a mining engineer in the Rosita mines.

Rosita's mining history began in Hardscrabble Canyon at the head of Grape Creek in 1863 with gold and silver discoveries by two brothers, Si and Stephen Smith. More was found in 1870 by Daniel Baker, and the Hardscrabble Mining District was born in November of 1872. By 1875 the population finally peaked at over 1,500 inhabitants, with close to five hundred houses and other buildings. Then there was a mine takeover attempt by two prominent residents named Walter Stuart and James Boyd, who hired a gun hand who was actually an escaped convict named Major Graham, plus they hired a gang of twenty ne'er-do-wells and saddle bums. These men took over a mine by force. However, this was Colorado, not back East, and one hundred angry citizens organized a vigilance committee called the Committee of Safety, and they took back the mine, scattered the entire gang, and shot and killed Graham the shootist. Walter Stuart stole all the money from the bank that he and his partner had started, and it turned out later that he was actually Walter C. Sheridan, one of America's most notorious bank robbers and forgers, and over the next several years the town died out, but eight miles away, Silver Cliff sprang up.

There were more mines, such as Edmund Bassick's large Bassick Mine, and the town of Querida had sprung up. Then, in the late seventies, the Bassicks sold most of their mine stock to a group of New York investors. Then scoundrels started stealing gold and silver ore from their absentee owners in New York and sold salted mines to unsuspecting people coming to the Wet Mountain Valley to seek their fortunes. Another vigilance committee was formed, secretly called the Querida Protective Society. They roughed up and threatened these crooks, making them leave the Wet Mountain Valley.

By June of 1880, over five thousand people had settled in the valley, and a thousand more prospected in the surrounding area. Silver Cliff was incorporated as a town in 1879. However, now the Denver and Rio Grande cut their way up and laid tracks in Grape Creek Canyon, and Westcliffe, just west of Silver Cliff, started growing by leaps and bounds as the Denver and Rio Grande Railroad ended its tracks on the edge of town. In fact, Dr. William Bell, the founder of Manitou Springs, and General Palmer, the founder of Colorado Springs, planned Westcliffe as the new town before the completion of the Denver and Rio Grande Railroad line.

Westcliffe began to thrive as a supply center for not only miners and tourists but for local ranchers and farmers as well. On top of that, several very large cattle herds started arriving in 1870, with Edwin Beckwith's herd of fifteen hundred Texas cattle. By 1880 there were over thirteen thousand head of cattle at ranches throughout Custer County.

By the time Zachariah Banta had finished telling the history of the Wet Mountain Valley area, Strongheart had already concluded that V. R. Clinton wanted to bring in the Atchison, Topeka and Santa Fe to compete with or replace the Denver and Rio Grande. Possibly he was going to bring in more cattle and try to start shipping by rail out of Westcliffe. Since his spread was well south of town, Joshua figured he might even want to expand the railroad down the valley, too, toward Alamosa.

He wanted to go reconnoiter the Clinton ranch, but first he had to find the Westcliffe Western Union office and send a telegram to Lucky, asking him to find out if Clinton had approached the senior officials of the Denver and Rio Grande about buying stock or becoming a partner. If he was turned down or snubbed, that might explain the reason for his financial investment in the railroad war. Joshua waited for a response and got one. Lucky was already ahead of him and had spoken to them. They had indeed turned down financial overtures by Clinton through his attorney out of Denver. The attorney was persistent and said his client did not take well to losing, ever.

Zach had to get back to Cotopaxi and Strongheart picked up a better map of the area showing V. R. Clinton's property. The two men shook hands and parted company.

10

THE FORTRESS

Strongheart took off, heading west from Westcliffe, then turned south, the thirteen- and fourteen-thousand-foot peaks of the Sangre de Cristo range towering before him in the sky. Clouds hovered over some of the majestic peaks, looking as if they were straining to break over from the western San Luis Valley side of the range. He would spend the night up high in the trees on Medano Pass, which crossed over the range into the San Luis Valley and into the Great Sand Dunes. He had been over this pass, located twenty-three miles south of Westcliffe, many times. The Great Sand Dunes was a large, 44,000-square-mile area right up against the mountain range made of fine sand with dunes that rose as high as 750 feet up into the air, constantly shifting, with a few streams of water that actually ran under and around them and, like the dunes, were always shifting course and location. The San Luis Valley was the largest high-mountain valley in the world, and the winds in the valley were such that the sands would come from dry areas of the Rio Grande at the southwestern end of the 50-by-150-mile, 8,000-foot-high desert valley and settle up against the twelve to fourteen thousand peaks in the southeastern portion of the valley. In fact, it would eventually become a national park.

On the eastern side of the range, Strongheart made camp later up in the trees overlooking the V. R. Clinton Ranch. He could see several thousand head of longhorn cattle grazing in the lush green pastures. The Wet Mountain Valley was fast becoming known for outstanding pastures and hay and alfalfa. Looking around the valley spread out before him in the late afternoon, Strongheart could see large harems of elk and large herds of mule deer with hundreds in each group grazing in several of the giant pastures.

When he set up camp, Strongheart made a large pile of rocks as a solid rest for the powerful binoculars he obtained from Zach Banta. He would use all available light to glass the ranch often and figure out his best route of approach. There was no information, no intelligence on V. R. Clinton, his ranch, or his plans, and Strongheart was bound and determined to find out more by sneaking in as close as he could to the main house, which was a large two-story stone building with a very large rock wall around it inside the sprawling ranch perimeter.

One thing he easily identified was ranch hands down below working the cattle and doing ranch chores, but there were others who looked to be vigilant and were obviously hired guns, not real cowboys.

He sat down after dark eating his supper and drinking coffee, then rolled up in his bedroll, looking at the stars and the snow-covered peaks of the range, such as Colony Peak and the distant Crestone Needles and Crestone Peak, as well as Marble Mountain, which has the Spanish Caves in an area up very high that is honeycombed with limestone caverns and connecting caves called the Caverna del Oro, or the Cavern of Gold, said to contain millions of dollars' worth of gold treasure left by the Spanish conquistadors.

Little did Joshua know a rider was aware of his intentions and was searching for him now, even after dark. The follower finally made camp himself, knowing it was insane to try to find the Pinkerton agent in the trees and rocks when he knew Joshua would make a camp that would not be easy at all to detect.

The follower also did not know that he was being followed as well. The follower made camp about one mile north of Strongheart, and his follower made camp about one mile north of him. Nobody seemed to want to let Strongheart know in the darkness how popular he had become, mainly because such a revelation might be met with a hail of bullets. The follower, knowing Strongheart would be awake before dawn, would awaken then and start moving at daybreak. He did not make a campfire, worried that Strongheart might see it during the night and sneak up on him. His follower was even more experienced in the wilderness than he was and did make a small, smokeless fire, snugly nestled in a small jumble of boulders that reflected the heat from the fire, blocked out any reflection, and filtered much of the little smoke there was. That watcher knew there was little chance he would be discovered by Joshua or anybody.

Shortly after daybreak, Strongheart crawled into the saddle and headed toward the ranch. He saw a gulch that was filled with scrub oak and went right up and through the large stone wall around the ranch and would provide excellent cover for his approach. However, he did not want to go that way, because it was the most obvious. There were two smaller gulches, also filled with vegetation, and neither went all the way to the wall. He could safely leave Eagle there without worry of him being spotted and sneak most of the way to the wall, and would then have to carefully low-crawl on his stomach for maybe three hundred feet, using selective cover.

Joshua Strongheart was now focused on the ranch below and the various activities going on; he was not watching his backtrail as carefully as he normally did. The follower was watching him with a small telescope and was now coming down off the mountain, following the same route Strongheart had used. However, his focus was on Strongheart, and he was not watching back up the mountain behind him, or he might have seen occasional glimpses of the second follower carefully putting the sneak on him. It took several hours for Joshua to get into position on the one draw so he could dismount, leave Eagle hidden out of sight in the trees, and move on by foot.

He dismounted and removed his boots and tied them with a leather thong to his saddle horn. He carefully, quietly removed the large-roweled spurs with two jingle-bobs on each and slid them into his saddlebags while he retrieved his moccasins and an extra .45 Peacemaker, tucking it into his belt in the back. He strung his bow and slipped it and his mountain lion–hide quiver full of arrows over his head and shoulder, wearing both diagonally on his back. The tall Pinkerton moved forward, Lakota style, walking slowly, toe first, then the heel.

He made no sound. With the quilled, soft-soled antelope-skin moccasins, Joshua could feel every pebble underfoot and would stop whenever his foot touched a stick. He would gingerly move his foot to another spot. When the undergrowth opened up, he would lie down on the ground, low-crawling forward, using his forearms and knees.

Strongheart was now close enough to the large stone wall he could literally throw a rock and hit it. The perspective was certainly different at ground level. It was, he estimated, ten feet in height.

The follower's large horse, like Eagle, was also trained to ground-rein, so he left him in the trees, and the two horses sniffed each other's noses, then calmly grazed in place, side by side. Removing his spurs, he pulled a pair of woolen socks over his boots, checked the bullets in his .44, and moved forward slowly, carefully. He had to close in to Joshua and hoped the wily Pinkerton agent would not spot him until he was almost upon him.

The other follower already had moccasins on and held back in the trees, watching the first follower, then stealthily, slowly moved forward.

Strongheart watched to his left, the north, and kept his eye on what looked like two legitimate cowhands roping, branding, and neutering bull calves. They also had a third cowhand, who was obviously another hired gun, not doing any work but sitting his horse, watching over the scene. Joshua pulled out his binoculars and observed the man for a while. With the two active cowhands, he knew he could sprint the last few yards and vault the ten feet up the wall and pull himself over. However, the gun hand was too watchful. Joshua had to figure out how to distract the man. He considered shooting a long, arching arrow and hoping when it struck it would make enough noise to distract him, but he knew he would have to aim at a spot so far away that the man would not even hear it strike.

He concluded he would inch his way forward on his belly all the way to the wall, moving so slowly the shootist would not see him. Then he would, like a lizard, grab the rocks with fingers and hands and work his way up to the top of the wall. Carefully watching the gunman, he slowly started moving forward. He knew at that distance he would not be very noticeable unless he moved quickly. Like a snail, Joshua inched along. It took him over an hour just to move several paces.

Reaching the wall, he started to lift himself up, ever so slowly, gripping with his fingers and the sides of his feet on the edges of stones. By now, the follower and the second follower were both in place in the trees watching, and both were amazed at his incredible strength to cling to the fingerholds in the rocks. It took a half an hour for Joshua to reach the top of the wall, then he had to slowly pull himself on top, where he lay perfectly still, all his muscles in his arms and legs shaking. He dared not move, though there could be people inside the compound below him watching him now or aiming guns at him. Joshua felt he had to simply take the risk and lie there until he recovered. Because he was in such excellent physical condition, it did not take long for him to do so.

Then, ever so slowly, he turned his head toward the inside of the wall and saw the large house. There before him, he saw her, totally nude, her long, golden hair hanging down around both shoulders, and she was grinning. Helena Victoria was standing in a second-floor bedroom staring at Joshua, wearing nothing but a large smile on her face. She did nothing to hide her nakedness, and Strongheart knew he had to think and move more quickly than she. He had to move fast and get back up into the trees, as she would call down the hounds of hell on him.

First she would have to put on a robe, at least, and he was already sprinting back toward the follower who was hidden in the treeline. The follower headed toward his horse as fast as he could move and vaulted into the saddle just as Joshua spotted him.

Strongheart said, "What are you doing here, and how did you get here?"

Scottie Middleton said, "I'll tell you when we are safe!"

Just then, Joshua heard a large bell clanging three times from the ranch compound. He knew instantly that it was a prearranged signal for help. He jumped up on Eagle, and they rode fast into the taller trees. The second follower was watching and was running fast ahead of them, retracing Joshua's trail back up the mountain.

Joshua was really puzzled at how Scottie had appeared and why. They rode well up into the trees and headed north along the front of the mountain range, following deer and elk trails at nine to ten thousand feet. Strongheart knew they could not push the horses like that, so he slowed Eagle to a walk for five minutes to cool him down, then finally stopped in an aspen grove and dismounted. Scottie followed suit.

They pulled canteens off their horses and drank deeply.

Joshua said, "Okay, tell me, Scottie, how did you find me, and why did you come after me?"

Scottie said, "I will, Joshua, but shouldn't we be running the horses farther? You know they have to have a lot of hands after us."

Strongheart said, "Maybe we should, but we need to let them have a blow and rest a little. They have been mainly staying down at five thousand feet. We are running them at twice the height. Sometimes, Scottie, you just have to give your horse a rest and stand and fight if you have to. Grab your rifle and make sure you have plenty of bullets."

With that, Joshua went over and grabbed his carbine, and Scottie grabbed his. They went back and sat down on logs. The other follower was catching up, but a hundred feet higher up the ridge.

Scottie said, "You know that woman you mentioned, Helena Victoria? Her real name is Victoria Roberta Clinton. V. R. Clinton is a she, not a he."

Joshua was amazed and said, "I just saw her through the upstairs window when I was on top of that wall and wondered what her connection was there, but how do you know, Scottie?"

"When I heard you and the sheriff talking about V. R. Clinton, I remembered Bernard Clinton at school," Scottie said. "Everybody ignores him, because he is strange, but I have always been nice to him. When you made me go to school, I talked to Bernard outside and asked him if he lived in Westcliffe. He said he does, but he lives down in Cañon City during the weeks we have school. His ma has money, he said, lots of it, and she didn't want him going to one of those one-room school-houses around Westcliffe. She sends him to Cañon City, and he stays with the Macons, Robesons, Adamics, or one of the main pioneer families. I can't remember which, but it don't matter."

Strongheart smiled, saying, "Doesn't matter."

"Yes, sir."

"Did you find out where she gets her money from?" Joshua asked.

"No," Scottie said.

"She got it from Robert Hartwell," a woman's voice said above them. "She was his woman."

Scottie and Strongheart both spun and drew their weapons to see the exquisitely beautiful cousin of Strongheart standing behind a tree above them. A paint horse followed her, and she carried a carbine and, like Joshua, wore a bow and a quiver of arrows on her back diagonally. She wore a doeskin dress that did little to hide all the curves in her body. Scottie immediately thought that she was the most beautiful Injun woman he had ever seen, then revised his thinking. Her face was the prettiest face he had ever seen on any woman.

Joshua holstered his pistol and said, "Cousin," as she rushed forward and threw herself into his arms.

He pushed her back and said, "I must be getting old or stupid. Both of you have put the sneak on me today. Scottie, this is my cousin Wiya Waste, which means 'beautiful woman.' Wiya Waste, this is my friend Scottie Middleton."

Scottie removed his hat and stammered, "A, um, pleased to meet you, ma'am."

She giggled and said, "My, what a handsome young warrior you are. My cousin has told me much about you."

"He has?" Scottie said, very well pleased.

He looked self-consciously at Joshua, who simply grinned.

Strongheart then got grim-faced. "Wiya, you live many days north of here at the circle of my father and his brother's wife, your mother. Why have you come here?"

He said it that way so Scottie would understand their relationship.

Wiya said, "I was told you seek V. R. Clinton, and I knew it was her. I cannot say her name good. Some of the chiefs learned this, that after you killed Hartwell, his woman took much money and came here. She has hair like the sun and long like a Lakota woman."

Joshua said, "You came all this way to tell me that?"

She said, "Yes, and to tell you what I have learned about Tȟašúŋke Witkó."

Scottie said, "Huh?"

Strongheart said, "I know how he was killed a few years ago. Is that what you mean?"

Scottie interrupted. "What do those words mean?"

Strongheart said, "Crazy Horse."

Scottie was excited. Just the name Crazy Horse sent many exciting images through his mind.

"What do you mean, cousin?" Strongheart asked.

"Crazy Horse was my father," she said, smiling.

"What?" he said. "How could that be?"

She said, "You know my mother was young when I was born?"

Joshua said, "Yes."

She went on. "Crazy Horse was young, too, and he and my mother loved each other, and he went away to fight with his own circle of teepees, the Oglala Lakota. Then, after he went away, I was born. My mother married your father's brother, who I thought was my father."

Strongheart said, "We need to talk about all this later, but how do you know?"

She said, "My mother, you know, has the coughing sickness now, and will soon die. She told me about it. . . . You are not my cousin, Joshua."

She looked at him, a hopeful look in her eyes, and moreso in her heart. She had loved this man since she was a little girl.

Strongheart was amazed and walked over to Eagle, picking up his reins and saying, "We'll talk later, but we need to get moving. I have many men after me by now, and I do not want to watch out for you two and try to stay alive at the same time. It does not work."

They mounted up and followed him as he zigzagged

through the trees. Unfortunately, that took just enough time for some of the gun hands to catch up. A shot rang out and Joshua squeezed Eagle's flanks, and they sprinted through the aspens, with Scottie and Wiya Waste close behind. More shots rang out behind them as they fled, but these were farther back. The aspens helped because they could only run on game trails used by deer and elk, with little fear of their pursuers spreading out behind them. They were running on the face of steep mountains with terrain rolling in and out of dips in gulches, and at a number of spots the horses leapt over fast-running, bubbling, churning whitewater glacial creeks roaring down the mountainside and spilling nature's lifeblood out into numerous channels lacing the Wet Mountain Valley floor below. Strongheart could see the many buildings of Westcliffe and even Silver Cliff off to his right front out across the valley many miles away. In less than thirty years, the game trails they were on would be made into a 110-mile-long north-to-south trail along the Sangre de Cristo range all the way down into New Mexico, and it would be called the Rainbow Trail, which would become a tourist attraction for hikers for over a century to come. For now, Joshua was just grateful the elk and deer had made these natural game trails across the face of each mountain.

He finally reined up and spun around to face the attackers, and then he saw what had happened. Wiya Waste was barely hanging on, holding her horse's mane in a tight grip. A giant bloodstain covered the upper right front of her dress, where a bullet had hit her back low in the right shoulder and passed through her body just above her right breast, but had fortunately missed her lungs. Joshua immediately knew this, because he saw no frothy bright red blood or bubbles coming out.

He called Scottie back and handed her reins to him, commanding, "Take her ahead and find us some boulders for cover."

She bravely forced a weak smile, but was barely awake. Scottie took off at a gallop, with her holding tight onto the mane of the paint mare. Strongheart faced their rear, his Colt Peacemaker in his right hand, carbine in the left.

In a minute's time, four riders appeared, rifles in their hands, but they were single file on the game trail. Joshua had pulled Eagle up with a large tree trunk along the trail between him and the pursuers. He aimed at the lead man, and his first shot went through the man's neck and hit the rider behind him on the left side of his face, blowing that side of his head off. He flew off his horse like a rag doll, slamming hard into a tree trunk and onto the ground, a bloody, lifeless mess. The other man dropped his rifle and clutched at his bloody throat, blood gurgling up out of the bullet hole, as his horse ran wildly off the trail and under a large maple tree branch, which hit the dying man in the chest, sending him backward.

Joshua knew that the accurate shooting and devastating results would play on the minds of his pursuers and make them more hesitant about coming after them too fast. He turned Eagle and took off after Scottie and Wiya Waste. Within ten minutes, he caught up and found that Scottie had indeed paid attention. He had made a camp amidst a large jumble of huge boulders, some the size of a small house. He had dismounted both horses and had Wiya lying on the ground with a clean cloth pressed against her wounds in both front and back.

Joshua dropped down, grabbing the Lakota beauty, and said, "Good job, son. Get up on that rock with a rifle and keep watch. I think I held them off for a while." He told Scottie not to look, and he carefully removed Wiya Waste's dress, built a small fire very quickly and stuck the point of his knife blade in it, then retrieved clean bandaging from his saddlebags and a pair of snipe-nosed pliers, which in modern day are called needle-nosed pliers. He had started carrying them for just such an emergency. He also stuck these in the fire, and he washed her wounds with canteen water, then added whiskey from a small flask he also carried in his saddlebags for wounds.

Upon cleaning her, he found that she'd had two bullets pass through the back of her shoulder. One tore through the front above her right breast, but the other stopped under the skin surface an inch higher and now created a large, angry bruise and a small lump under the skin where it had not broken through.

Joshua handed her the whiskey flask and said, "Take one quick swallow."

Then he stuck a green stick in her mouth and said, "Bite down!"

She bit the stick and he asked, "Are you ready?"

Eyes opened wide in fear, she nodded yes.

Strongheart quickly and efficiently cut through the lump where the bullet pushed against her skin. She bit down hard and was clearly in pain, but did not make a sound. He grabbed the snipe-nosed pliers and reached into the bloody hole, grabbing the bullet and pulling it out the front. She clearly almost fainted from the pain and breathed very heavily, but never let out as much as a whimper.

He then poured whiskey on the bloody wound and, following that, wrapped her shoulder and covered the wounds with bandaging. Wiya Waste spit out the stick and reached up with her arm and pulled Strongheart to her lips, kissing him fully. He kissed her back. Joshua quickly pulled her dress back on her and helped her stand. She still wore her porcupine-quilled moccasins, almost identical to Joshua's. She had made his for him.

"Can you ride?" he asked.

She smiled, saying, "I am Lakota. I am the daughter of Crazy Horse, an Ogle Tanka Un of the Lakota." (A term meaning "shirt wearer," a war chief.)

He grinned.

He literally lifted her up and set her on her pinto mustang. Joshua vaulted into his own saddle, and Scottie, wanting to emulate the flash and dash of his mentor, jumped from the top of his boulder, landing in the saddle of his black Thoroughbred, Hero. They went up higher into the mountains, heading for the timberline to find a hideout and make camp. Joshua thought of the perfect place. They moved north fast, heading for Hermit Peak. Lake San Isabel was beneath it, right below the timberline, with heavy forest to the west and high, steep peaks all around it to the north, east, and south. They could hide in there, have plenty of game, fish, and make a good camp where a fire would not be seen. Their fire and camp could only be spotted from the steep, snowcapped slopes above them, and no horsemen were going to journey up there.

They made it there a few hours before dark and left their pursuers far behind, jumping at every shadow. Seeing the destruction Strongheart caused by killing just a few of the pursuers really made believers out of those who were there. They saw Strongheart's shooting prowess. Seeing someone bounce off a tree with a sickening *thud* impacted their psyche even more. They now were twenty strong, but moving very slowly across the mountainside. On top of that, Strongheart had had Scottie go back and wipe out their tracks several times with large branches.

Joshua was very impressed with Wiya Waste's tenacity and fortitude. She had clung to the mane hair of her pinto while he led it with a long lead line attached to its Lakota war bridle. She mainly held on with her muscular legs clinging to the horse's sides.

Strongheart led them along the lake, then through

the big trees, and found a great place to make camp at the edge of the forest. The peaks rose up around them on all sides, and across the lake, Hermit Peak towered over them. Scottie got busy helping Joshua make camp, but was amazed at the speed and efficiency with which Strongheart worked. They cut large, thick evergreen branches and made a comfortable bed for Wiya Waste, then Joshua carried her to the bed of boughs, covered her with his saddle roll, and gently laid her down. She kept trying to get up to help, but Joshua would not let her. He got large rocks and put them in a circle about three feet across to build a campfire. While he did this, Scottie grabbed dry logs to burn and squaw wood.

Joshua got a fire going and put water on to heat up.

He said, "They are not going to move very fast, and may send for a tracker if they have one at the ranch. We don't have to be too careful . . . yet. Scottie, I am going to clean Wiya Waste's wound better, and I want you to fetch us cattails, wild rose, buck brush, wheatgrass, some fresh green oak branches—I need the sap—and if you can find any elderberries or blueberries, grab a bunch, a hatful, and some skunk cabbage. Do you know all those plants?"

Scottie said, "Yes, sir, I shore do. Gathered 'em all at one time or t'other with my aunt. But why do you need all of them?"

Wiya Waste interjected, "He makes a poultice for my wounds and some food to help me in case I get bad red color and fire."

Joshua grinned. "She is talking about infection and fever."

She smiled and said, "I do not speak American well, but I will learn. I must. Our days are over."

Scottie hopped up on Hero and took off around the lake, and in the meantime, Joshua looked around the lakeshore and found a large, flat rock with a dimpled center. He carried it back to the campsite and set it down, then washed it off with hot water. He returned to the shoreline and finally found an oblong stone, rounded on all sides. He returned to the camp and cleaned it off, too. Then he let the fire fry the two stones.

He removed Wiya Waste's dress again, secretly marveling at her natural beauty. He re-cleaned and re-dressed her wounds and left her dress off, covering her naked body with his slicker, which he kept rolled up with his bedroll. As he covered her, she looked at him longingly.

The Lakota beauty said, "Kiss me."

Joshua said, "No. You rest."

He smiled softly. Strongheart knew if he kissed her, he would not want to stop, now knowing that she was not his cousin. He also knew that he had to be extremely careful, because they were hiding in the wilderness, miles away from any civilization, well above ten thousand feet high, almost to the timberline, in fact. The chances of her getting a bad infection were great, and if she did, they would really be in trouble. Joshua knew that the pursuers had been told in no uncertain terms to kill him. Victoria had been found out, and he held her secret, and she knew he would tell those with him. She did not want him getting back to civilization, and when they realized he had two with him, they would want to kill them, too. She had been the recipient of Robert Hartwell's ill-gotten millions. This woman was ruthless, as Joshua had learned when she slipped him a Mickey the first night they met.

Scottie arrived after an hour with all the ingredients Joshua had asked for, and Strongheart soon was using the rounded oblong stone on the large flat one, rolling the smaller over the larger to extract seeds, juice, or sap from the vegetation he laid out on the bottom stone.

Scottie said, "What are you doing, Joshua?"

Wiya Waste said, "He uses a *wiyukpan* to make medicine from *hutkhan* for Wiya Waste. I do not know the words."

"Huh?" Scottie said.

Strongheart rolled hard on some cattails, squishing and pulverizing them, and chuckled, saying, "Wiya Waste is saying that I am using a grinder to grind up roots to make her medicine. *Wiyukpan* means 'grinder,' and *hutkhan* means 'roots,' like tree or plant roots. The Lakota use rocks like this the way a pharmacist uses a mortar and pestle to make drugs for you at a pharmacy."

"That is neat," Scottie said. "I wish I could speak another language, too."

"Go to school," Joshua said. "My mother knew it would be hard for me because I am half-red and half-white, so she made sure I went to school a lot. I went through college."

"His mother was a very wise woman," Wiya Waste said. "She brought him many times to our village to learn the ways of his father, but she also wanted him to know the ways of the white man. Wanji Wambli knows many things."

Scottie replied, *"Wanji Wambli?"*

She replied, "One Eagle. He comes from two flocks of birds. One flock is red birds and one flock is white birds. He is one bird, but he is one eagle, and flies alone."

Strongheart spent an hour grinding roots while Scottie went in search of more cattails and other edibles for dinner. Joshua made a poultice and placed it over Wiya Waste's wounds. She seemed to relax afterward.

It was almost dark now, and Joshua grabbed his bow and arrows and left as Scottie started a pot of stew. Joshua headed toward the lake farther north, traveling through the trees. He wore his moccasins and soon came upon a lone younger mule deer buck grazing on the rich grasses in a break in the trees.

Strongheart reached down while still keeping his eyes on the buck. He had seen several thistles and pulled the top off of one. Bringing it slowly to his lips, he blew, and the thistles blew directly from his left to his right. That was just what he wanted. He nocked an arrow on the string and slowly moved forward, watching not the deer's head, but his tail.

Mule deer, white-tailed deer, and even black-tailed deer in America all have the same type of vision, which Native Americans learned through centuries of trial and error. They had rods and cones in their vision, so could see the ground directly in front of them but nothing in their peripheral vision. They also could not see anything that was not moving, so if the wind was right, Joshua could sneak in close to the buck, no matter how near, as long as he was silent and froze in place whenever the deer raised its head. As long as the wind did not shift, he would watch the deer's tail, because a nerve in the tail would make it twitch very, very slightly a split second before the deer raised its head. If Joshua saw the tail twitch and his foot was in the air stepping forward, he would freeze, holding his body perfectly still until the deer put its head back down to graze some more.

When Joshua would go to his father's village as a boy and a young man, he would sometimes go out with younger braves, and they would challenge each other to see who could stalk closest to a deer or elk. He usually won. One thing he learned that was very important was that deer seemed to see shiny things very easily. For that reason, Strongheart had tucked his Colt Peacemaker into the back of his gun belt. He also learned as a boy that sometimes when he got close to deer, they could see themselves in their own reflection off his eyeballs. He learned when he got very close to squint, so they could not see the shine. Twice he had literally reached out and touched the side of the hindquarters of mule deer does.

In both cases, he got kicked, once cutting his skin over a rib, and he ended up with a painful little bruise on the rib from the powerful legs and tiny hooved feet.

He moved until he was within twenty feet of the deer, and when it put its head down, he drew his arrow. He held the string with three fingers, as always, and put his bent right thumb up against his jaw on the right side, kept both eyes open, took a breath and let it halfway out, and held his aim slightly over the deer's rump and to the right of him. The arrow struck true and entered low behind the buck's left shoulder, slicing through the meat and its heart, nicking the right lung as it went out the right side of its chest. It jumped up, kicking both hind legs, and ran in bounding leaps into the trees along the lakeside, and Joshua saw it fall not much beyond that.

Wiya Waste and Scottie sat in front of a small, crackling fire with vegetables, cattail roots, and dandelions cooking on a small pot that Scottie had carried with him. Joshua walked out of the trees with the small buck, field dressed, over his broad right shoulder.

He said, "Now we have some nice meat."

They both smiled, and he immediately cut them backstraps off the deer and started cooking them over the fire. As he had been taught, Scottie had stuck two green, forked sticks into the ground on both sides of the fire, with a sharpened green stick over the fire, sitting in the notches of the forked sticks. Joshua impaled the backstraps with these.

The three were enjoying the meal and cups of coffee,

and Wiya Waste grinned, saying, "Now, if all the bad men come and kill us, our stomachs will be happy."

This remark really struck Strongheart's fancy. Maybe because he was exhausted and all he had been through, he started laughing, which made him laugh even harder, and soon all three were laughing uproariously. Then it hurt Wiya Waste to laugh, and she moaned, and this made Scottie and Joshua laugh even more, and she of course joined in. All three sat around the campfire, tears rolling down their cheeks.

All of a sudden the three stopped, and Scottie suddenly said seriously, "I did not know that Indians laughed. I always thought you were so serious."

Joshua and the beautiful Sioux woman looked at each other, and both started laughing even more at Scottie's innocent remark. Joshua had not laughed so hard in years, and literally fell backward off the stump he had been sitting on.

11

THE BATTLE

During the brief time that Strongheart, Scottie, and Wiya Waste were in the Wet Mountain Valley and the Sangre de Cristo mountains, a lot had happened. The Denver and Rio Grande Railroad had essentially won the railroad war in court when the court found in their favor over the Atchison, Topeka and Santa Fe Railway. Several skirmishes took place at the AT&SF garrisons in Colorado, in both Denver and Colorado Springs. Doc Holliday and Bat Masterson's headquarters were in Pueblo, where gunfighters held out the longest, but they eventually accepted defeat. Doc and Bat and a few of the gun hands headed up to Westcliffe to get their final pay, and Victoria's new go-between ranch foreman, Swede Johansen, told them about Joshua and the other two running and hiding out in the folds of the purple-and-green mountain range. Of course, he neglected to say that one was a Sioux Indian woman and the other was a teenaged boy. What he said was that Joshua and two cohorts sneaked in, climbed up the wall around the ranch complex, and tried to dry-gulch V. R. Clinton, firing at him through the windows with rifles and shotguns.

Now there were twenty-three men searching for Joshua Strongheart and his companions, and the group was headed by Bat Masterson and Doc Holliday. The entire group had returned to the ranch headquarters, and there they met up with Doc and Bat. They told where they had searched so far, but they were waiting for a Mountain Ute Indian tracker named Fancy Moccasins, who was wearing very modest, plain, dirty elk-hide moccasins. He was a noted tracker and told Swede he could indeed find three people, no matter how hard they tried to hide their trail.

After the ones who had returned pointed at the big range and explained where they had already searched, Doc commented to Swede, "Ah do believe, suh, that this altitude is definitely not conducive to my prolonged health and well-being. In fact, the altitude here in West-cliffe has been horrible for my current medical inconvenience. Therefore, I shall go down to a lower elevation and await more news, maybe at a faro table in Pueblo. Mah good friend Bat Masterson heah will know how to find me, if Ah'm needed. In fact, there is a hotel on the west end of Cañon City with some delightful medicinal hot springs. I do believe I shall go there instead and soak up some of that good natural medicine and see if they have any good faro games in the evening. I met Mr. Strongheart and have very strong reservations about him bushwhacking anybody. In fact, if you continue pursuing him, I can guarantee that a good many of you will not be returning. Good hunting, gentlemen."

Bat shook hands with him, and Doc turned his horse, heading toward distant Westcliffe. As he rode away, the group watched the frail gunfighter and sporting man, as he called himself, several in the group sensing they were witnessing and had been riding, however briefly, with one who was to become a Western legend. Swede wanted to challenge Doc's comments about not believing that Strongheart was a dry-gulcher, but he thought better of it. More than one person had raised the former dentist's ire, and they soon learned how proficient he actually was with both pistols and his hidden knife. That took place earlier in the day.

After Joshua and Wiya Waste stopped laughing at a chuckling, embarrassed Scottie's expense, Strongheart explained, "The Lakota, just like white people, love to laugh, to love, to have families, enjoy their children, eat good meals, you name it."

Scottie said, "Never thought about things like that."

Joshua said, "Unfortunately, most people don't."

Joshua put a couple of logs on the fire and said, "We better get some sleep. Tomorrow we'll need to be more careful. They will eventually find us, but I do not want Wiya Waste to move yet. She lost a lot of blood, and I don't want her to get an infection."

Scottie said, "Good night."

Strongheart said, "Night, Scottie."

Wiya Waste said, "Good night."

Scottie said, "Mr. Strongheart—I mean, Joshua—do we need to take turns keeping watch?"

The Pinkerton replied, "No, not tonight. The horses will let us know if anybody comes along before they get here. Most of the breezes are coming from downhill toward us, and with the high cliffs, the horses will hear voices and hooves echoing from a long ways off."

Scottie used his saddle as a pillow and lay down on his slicker, covering up with his blanket roll.

Meanwhile, Strongheart pleasantly surprised Wiya Waste, as he lay down next to her, covering both of them with the blanket, and laid her head on his massive arm. There was no place in the world she would rather be.

Joshua said, "Scottie, I have all my clothes on and am just lying here to help keep her warm tonight so she can get rest."

Scottie had his back to both of them, and said, "Yes, sir," while grinning to himself.

All Wiya Waste ever wanted her entire life was to be held by those massive arms and lay her head on that muscular chest. She felt so protected in Joshua's grasp, and she knew the odds of her dying from such a wound. She thought that if she did die now, her life was complete anyway, because she was finally in Joshua's embrace, her lifelong passion.

At the same time, Strongheart was thinking about how horrible he had felt for months after the gruesome death of Annabelle Ebert, his fiancée. He thought about how much he beat himself up for not being able to protect her from the horrible multiple murderer Blood Feather. He knew that Wiya Waste had come on her own to bring him news about Victoria Clinton, but he still felt an obligation to protect her and do everything in his power to shield her from death somehow. He simply could not bear thinking about losing another woman he loved.

Then he thought about Brenna Alexander in Chicago. She was wealthy, beautiful, passionate, successful, and well-groomed, and she was madly in love with him. He thought about how impossible a marriage to Wiya Waste would be. She, like his father, was a full-blooded Lakota and grew up as part of a tribal circle, with different beliefs, daily habits, and societal mores. He could live among his father's people and be happy, but he was a Pinkerton agent. That was his career, and he was passionate about it. He could not live among the People permanently. He pictured Belle again and thought about how much he had missed her. He suddenly felt guilty. Although he was fully clothed, Wiya Waste was naked under the blanket, and he felt her soft skin where it touched his arms and neck. He had bathed her, and she smelled of soap and of woman. He drifted off to sleep with this beautiful Sioux woman, the daughter of Crazy Horse, almost purring with her head on his chest and his arm around her.

Joshua's eyes opened, and he reached for his Peacemaker and slowly, quietly drew it from his holster. Eagle was restless. Strongheart looked at Wiya Waste beside him, and her eyes were wide open.

She whispered, "I heard your horse, too."

He whispered, "Put your dress and moccasins on, quietly, slowly. Do you need my help?"

"No," she whispered.

He just lay there, watching, listening.

The big silvertip grizzly had been a mile away when a quick wind shift brought a world of information to his nostrils and his brain. He caught the smell of their fire, her soap, the rifles and pistols and the gunpowder, the hanging deer carcass, the vegetables they ate, the coffee, and the horses. His mind cataloged all these smells, and the bear instinctively knew the deer was dead. He was standing on his hind legs again and could see the dim fire from the camp. Joshua saw his outline against the moonlit surface of the lake. He was now a dark shadow just standing up and testing the wind. It had shifted toward them. To get downwind, he would have to circle around, but would have to climb one of the cliffs surrounding them. The human smell brought a memory. Two years earlier, in the bear's fourth summer, he was outside a ranch near Poncha Springs. He was eating afterbirth in the spring, which bears loved to do, and was able to catch a newly born calf and break its neck with one quick bite. He was feeding when suddenly he smelled that man smell for the first time, and there was a loud explosion as the rancher shot. The bullet hit a rock under his left foreleg, but it splintered and a sliver went into his front leg and partially into his knee joint. It was painful at times, as it moved around in and out of the joint, but it served as a reminder that the man smell brought pain and loud noise. The boar was salivating, but the fear of man smell overpowered his instinct to gather easy food. He dropped to all fours and sauntered away, skirting the lake, and followed the wind coming into his face. He would travel fifteen more miles north before lying down and feeding off the rotting carcass of a lightning-struck elk.

Without a word other than Joshua saying, "He left," the two fell asleep again, but not before he thought about how impressed he was that she awakened, too, at the horses' soft nickering. Strongheart was very glad her clothes were back on.

He dreamed and saw Belle Ebert floating down off a cloud and into his arms. They kissed and made love, but then he opened his eyes and she was gone, and Brenna Alexander was lying there, and they kissed and he opened his eyes, and Wiya Waste was lying there, smiling up into his face. Then, all three appeared before him and started arguing with each other. They all walked up into the cloud still arguing, and Strongheart awakened, frustrated.

He got up and checked on the horses, then built up the fire. Joshua was going through the pile of firewood, pulling out some pieces of wood and tossing them aside. Scottie got up, and so did Wiya Waste, who started making breakfast.

Scottie said, "Joshua, why are you throwing some of the sticks and logs off into another pile?"

Joshua said, "We could see the bad men today, but we do not have to make their job easier. We want a smokeless fire. Now, we can't really have it smokeless, but I am sorting out the wood that causes more smoke. I also picked this spot so there are trees nearby that will filter a lot of the smoke before it gets up into the sky."

Scottie said, "I never thought of that."

Strongheart replied, "Think about the times you have been out in the prairie and saw campfire smoke from miles away."

Scottie said, "Yeah, it is very easy to spot."

Strongheart said, "So, if you are in that spot, you want to make a smaller fire and be sure you use very dry wood, usually with the bark off, that is older, with no greenness to it."

"Yes, sir," Scottie responded.

He saddled his horse and grabbed his rifle.

Strongheart said, "Where are you going?"

Scottie said, "To scout down the canyon a little and make sure nobody's coming yet."

Joshua said, "I think you should stay here, Scottie. Too dangerous."

Scottie laughed and said, "We have a bunch of killers looking for us. There's you, and there's me, a teenaged boy, and a wounded woman, a Sioux woman, who is probably better with her bow and arrows than her rifle, and she can't shoot the bow because she is shot up. You want me to stay here because it is too dangerous?"

Wiya Waste started laughing, and Strongheart chuckled himself.

"Guess if you want to be a man, I should let you," Joshua said.

Wiya said, "Why do you not wait, Scottie, and eat first? The food is ready."

He sat down with the other two, and they ate breakfast and drank coffee. Joshua said, "Make sure you both drink plenty of water this morning, too. We don't know how much we might be running and moving today."

Scottie thanked the beauty and mounted up, galloping off into the trees. Strongheart was glad the boy was using his head, not exposing himself by riding the easy way around the lake. He could hear him breaking branches as he went through the trees.

He poured two more cups of coffee, and he and Wiya Waste sat down by the fire.

"I have to get you to a hospital," he said. "Your wound looks angry in the front and the back."

"What does this mean?" she replied.

"It means it has become infected," Joshua said. "It can kill you if we do not take care of it."

"My friend's mother died because of a small wound that got infected," she said. "I understand. The white men will not let me go to their hospital."

"Oh yes, they will," he said. "I will make sure of that."

She felt proud hearing him say that, as he was being protective of her. She would never forget being able to sleep on his arm all night.

Strongheart said, "There is an Indian hospital in Oklahoma, but I am taking you to the hospital in Denver where I stayed when I was attacked by a grizzly and when I got shot up in Florence."

"How will you make them let me be there?" she asked.

Strongheart said, "Trust me. I will."

She smiled and took a sip of coffee, which she loved with cream and sugar, but which only had sugar right now.

"We must get ready to go," Strongheart said.

She immediately pulled out her rifle and started cleaning it.

Joshua said, "You won't need that. Scottie and I will be doing the shooting. I am more worried about you being able to stay on your horse."

She set her rifle down and walked over to Joshua, looked around, and said, "Wanji Wambli, Scottie is not here, so you listen to me now. My words are iron! I love you, Joshua. I have since I was a little girl, but I am not your baby girl. I am a woman. I am Lakota! I am the daughter of Crazy Horse. I am a warrior, and it is time to fight. We have many enemies today, and this is a good day to die. If I die, I die with the man I love. But do not treat me like I am weak. I am hurt, but I am a warrior, and I will fight and I will count many coup this day. Do you understand?"

Joshua grinned, saying, "Yes, ma'am."

They struck the camp and mounted up. At the end of the canyon, Scottie carefully moved his horse forward. He heard a stone roll down a steep ridge at one point, and he heard one tree branch crack in the distance. Before him the trail narrowed significantly, and it seemed a perfect place for any ambush. He clutched his carbine a little more tightly as he moved toward the squeeze point. Where the trail suddenly narrowed there was thick foliage on both sides, mainly from a scrub oak thicket and stunted cedars. Next to the trail was a large, hollowed-out tree stump that had obviously been exploded by lightning years before. It stood about ten feet high.

As he inched into the closing, he could hear his heart pounding in his ears, and felt it pounding in his temples and the sides of his neck. His ears and eyes strained to detect the slightest movement, the slightest sound. He heard some little tiny birds tweeting a few feet away in the morass of green, but could not see them and couldn't identify them by their sound. His breathing became difficult, and his head felt to him like it had been filled up with mud. Just as he passed the dead tree, there was an explosion, and Scottie jumped in the saddle, startled out of his wits. He cried out, and the red-tailed hawk he had startled almost flew into his face as it took off from its perch on the limb on the opposite side of the dead tree. It quickly flew up over the treetops and disappeared to the north, and Scottie laughed at himself for getting so nervous and then so scared when the predator spooked.

The weight of Fancy Moccasins's body hit Scottie full force from the left, the tracker's arms wrapping around the teenager's arms as the pair flew into the greenery on the right side of the trail. They hit the ground, and the tracker's body forced the air out of Scottie. Then he felt other hands grab him, powerful ones, and he felt his rifle being yanked away and his pistol being pulled from his holster. He started to yell for Strongheart, but a ham-sized fist smashed him in the mouth, bloodying and swelling both lips. The world was spinning, and he felt himself being dragged to his feet, and was now being tied up with rope.

Minutes later, Scottie was in the custody of two dozen armed thugs. Someone kicked him in the ribs, and he panicked. It bruised two ribs, but also kicked the wind out of him, and he struggled to try to breathe.

Someone put a rope around his neck and tightened

the noose while the other end was thrown over a branch, and he realized he was about to be lynched.

Somebody asked, "Where's his horse, that big black?"

Another man said, "He took off when the tracker jumped him."

He was placed on the back of a bright red sorrel mustang with no saddle, only a rope halter and lead line around his head. A calm came over Scottie, and he got angry now. His lips and mouth were bleeding, it was painful to breathe each breath, and he was mad that he was about to die and had not fought back at all.

One of the gunslingers, a very tall black cowboy with twin Colt Peacemakers, butts forward in cross-draw holsters, said in a deep, low voice, "Where is Strongheart, boy?"

Scottie stuck out his chin and said, "You can go to hell!"

Someone behind him said, "Thet's where yer going in about one minute, buster."

The black cowboy said, "I will ask you one more time. If you tell me, we will hang you fast and let your neck snap, but if you don't tell me, we will pull you up and let the rope strangle you real slow. Where is Strongheart?"

Scottie thought quickly and laughed heartily, then said, "Probably aiming at your head right now with his Sharps."

Strongheart had told him that when your life is on

the line, lying doesn't count and you should always try to buy time. Set your enemy off balance; make them worry.

He could see the worry now.

Scottie said, "He is watching, and you lynch me, he'll open fire and kill all of you. If you let me go, he probably will let some of you go. You kill me, and he might set these woods on fire. Any of you ever seen Strongheart in a gun battle? You ever heard about his shootouts?"

They were thinking now. Scottie knew his horse would run back to join his pasture buddy, Eagle. That was the nature of horses. They are herd animals. They hate to be alone, and Hero had been spooked by the hawk and then the ambush, just like Scottie was. He was right—the big black ran into Joshua along the lake's edge.

Strongheart said, "Grab his reins and follow me. I have to fast track this horse back. Scottie is in trouble."

Wiya Waste said, "Go."

She caught Hero, tied his reins to her horse's tail, and led him forward, her rifle across the front of her saddle. She wanted both hands free in case she had to shoot.

The gang members looked around nervously, picturing a man like Joshua Strongheart with a Sharps buffalo gun in his hand. By the early 1880s, the long-range 1874 Sharps in .45/.70 caliber had become the favorite rifles of buffalo hunters and mountain men. Many shooters had practiced at targets one thousand feet away with the

Sharps, and Joshua's legendary reputation really made these men nervous. In actuality, he had his Winchester in his hand and could draw his pistols when he wanted.

He fast-trotted forward until he saw the trail narrow well ahead of him, and he had to chance that Scottie had been ambushed there. It was too obvious a spot. He pulled Eagle off the trail into the trees and knew that Wiya Waste would find his horse there. Joshua grabbed his bow, arrows, and rifle, switched back to his moccasins, and headed into the trees at a run.

The black cowboy said, "Maybe we should keep him alive and tie him up to a tree. Strongheart will come for him eventually, and we will be hiding all around. Tie him up to that tree, boys, and find a hiding spot."

Two men bound Scottie to a large elm tree with ropes, his arms outstretched backward on the large tree. They quickly went into the trees looking for a hiding place, each feeling grateful that the lead shooter had listened to Scottie's reasoning. It was bad enough facing Strongheart as a group, but if they really had to feel his full wrath, many more might perish. They also pictured him one thousand yards off picking out targets and then making their heads explode with a Sharps buffalo gun he did not really have.

On his powerful arms and legs, Strongheart low-crawled into position. He had already picked out three targets, and one was the leader. He drew two arrows from his quiver and nocked a third one on the bow. He aimed at the black gunfighter, checked on the other two targets, drew the arrow back to the anchor point under the back of his right jaw, took a breath, let it halfway out, and released the arrow. He was already nocking the second arrow as he saw the leader fall forward, a hole through his forehead where the arrow had entered, and it exited his skull in the back.

The second target was a redheaded little man wearing a pair of Colt Navy .36s. Joshua's arrow went into the man's chest, through his lung and upper torso, and lodged against a rib in his back. He jumped up with a panicked look on his face and was frantically pulling at his shirt in the front where the arrow went through it, frothy bubbles already pouring out of his mouth and spilling onto his chest. Joshua had to waste his third arrow on him to put him down, and a second arrow sliced through the man's chest. He fell forward, dead.

Strongheart quickly pulled another arrow from his quiver, nocked it, and drew as he saw the third man, another black gunfighter, draw his gun, spotting Joshua's hiding place between two bushes thirty paces away. The Pinkerton released the arrow, and it passed through the man's Adam's apple and his neck, sliced his cervical vertebrae, and paralyzed him instantly. He fell to the ground, immobile, and started choking on his own blood. His heart almost exploded from sheer panic and terror, but soon stopped beating anyway.

Strongheart low-crawled from his position, confident

the others in hiding could not see the ground out in front of Scottie. With Scottie simply brimming with renewed hope and confidence now, Joshua quickly low-crawled up to him, and reached up with his knife.

Joshua whispered, "When I cut your ropes, hold your arms and legs there like you're still tied, until I get a horse and some guns for you."

"They hid the horses to my right. See that pine thicket?"

Joshua replied, "Yes. Back in there?"

"Yes," Scottie said. "I knew you would come. They were gonna lynch me, Joshua. How'd you find me so quick?"

Strongheart said, "Hero was a hero."

He crawled off toward the thicket. In there, he found a horse still saddled and bridled, a gun belt hanging from the saddle horn, and a rifle in the scabbard, running under the right stirrup. Strongheart swung up on the big steed, put his heels to him, and galloped out of the thicket and to Scottie. As he reached the young man, he stretched out with his right hand, and he grabbed Scottie's forearm while Scottie grabbed Strongheart's forearm and swung easily up behind him. Shots started ringing out as they raced away.

Bullets whistled all around them, and one hit a tree trunk right by them. They made it to Eagle, and Joshua jumped onto his own saddle, grabbed the reins, and started to race back toward Wiya Waste. However, she came racing out of the trees to his left, Hero trailing behind her. Her face was drawn and pale, and Strongheart was worried that her infection had worsened. He rode up to her and felt her forehead, and it was hot. She had a fever. He pulled the top of her dress aside, and the wound in front was red and angry outside the bandages. He *had* to get her to a hospital.

Then, he turned and saw blood running down the side of Scottie's arm. He ran over to him and saw a large bullet crease running along Scottie's triceps on his left arm.

Joshua said, "Did you get shot riding behind me?"

Scottie said, "Yes, sir, but I didn't want to bother you with it."

Strongheart said, "I swear!"

He pulled Scottie's kerchief off and bound the wound, saying, "You okay?"

Scottie said, "Let me at them," as he jumped up on Hero.

Strongheart said, "Scottie, you see that peak up there? It is not as high as most. It's only twelve thousand feet, and most of the other peaks are fourteen thousand feet, and rockier. You can go up there and drop over on the north side of the peak and down into the San Luis Valley. You will see the town of Del Norte when you are up on top. You just ride across the valley or stop at any of the ranches, and they can get you back to Cañon City. There is a good chance Wiya Waste and I will get killed, but I cannot wait any longer. We're going to fight our way out of here, head across the valley and down to the railroad in Cañon City. I have to get her to a hospital right away, or she will die."

Scottie said, "Joshua, Mr. Strongheart, yer my boss, and I do what I'm told, but there is no way you can make me leave you and Wiya Waste."

Joshua looked at Wiya Waste, and she grinned at him while he shook his head.

He looked at her intensely and said, "We have to do this. You understand that?"

She smiled, saying, "We will make it."

He said, "White men usually use one name for people, so since today is Wednesday and that sounds something like Wiya Waste, I'm going to start calling you Wednesday. Then, like with the doctor or at the hospital, we will say your name is Wednesday. Okay?"

She smiled weakly, obviously in a lot of pain now, and said, "I like the name."

Scottie said, "I like it, too."

A lead horseman appeared from the shootists, and Strongheart lifted his rifle and fired before the man could even think to raise his own. He fell back on his horse's rump, did an unplanned backward somersault, and was kicked squarely in the face by his horse's right hoof. He was dead when he hit the ground.

Strongheart said, "Now they know exactly where we are, so we will go around the woods over there and will be on their east side. Maybe the trees will even get us around some of them. Let's go."

They ran toward the base of one of the surrounding peaks, and the bright sunlight shimmering off the snow-caps felt like it was only a few feet above them. The horses trotted through the trees and around their eastern edge, which rose up on several ridges. This worked to their advantage for almost an hour, but finally they saw a blocking force waiting for them about one hundred yards ahead or better.

Joshua immediately knew that blocking force had to be a tactical maneuver to get them to run westward into the trees. Instead he spun Eagle and rode past Wednesday and Scottie.

He yelled, "Follow me!"

He ran back the way they had come, knowing that the large force would not plan for that, since they were figuring he would surely head into the trees to seek an alternate route out of the canyon. After fifteen minutes of hard riding, they were back to their starting point, and he reined Eagle to the right and headed due north, right up through the middle of the forest.

He had calculated correctly. Within minutes, he saw off to their right the movement of ambushers who had been waiting for him to run right into them. They were scrambling to get to their horses while the trio headed toward the mouth of the canyon. At one point, he reined in and held his hand up.

He turned and explained, "We have to take it easy on our horses, or we will kill them."

Gunfire suddenly opened up behind them, and they

had no choice but to run toward the canyon opening. Once there, they would turn east and head down the mountainside, looking for a low, tree-covered ridge to provide plenty of cover. At some point they would have to stop and make a stand and rest the horses, so Joshua kept looking for that. Twice he stopped, spun Eagle around, and shot riders out of their saddles—three of them. The gang of killers was now down to about fifteen.

Strongheart made the end of the high-mountain canyon and headed into an avalanche chute off to their right, but soon saw it had too many knocked-down trees to dodge, so he moved to their left, up onto the next ridgeline. It was a more gentle slope, and, being at the top of a ridge, the trees were not quite as thick. He dashed forward on his horse, and he kept worrying about Wednesday's. It was a Lakota mustang and an unknown quantity. He knew Hero could keep up and was sure-footed and long-winded, but he did not know how long the mustang could last running, especially downhill, which was harder on a horse's legs than any other activity.

The worry was taken away from Strongheart when Scottie yelled, "Joshua!"

The Pinkerton spun around and saw that Wiya Waste's horse had taken a round through the head and was falling face-first, dragging its head in the dirt as it went down. Somehow, Wiya Waste was on her feet, staggering and apparently dazed, and the fusillade of bullets increased. Joshua signaled Scottie to come forward fast, and he took careful aim at the fast-approaching horsemen in the woods and unloaded his carbine into them with accurate, withering rapid fire. There was no way Wednesday could grab his forearm to swing herself up in the saddle. She looked totally dazed.

He shoved his rifle into his scabbard, dug his heels into Eagle, and yelled, "Heeyah!"

The big black-and-white horse leapt forward, his powerful muscles bunching and lunging under Strongheart's own powerful legs, which were now clinging tightly to the horse's ribs. Wednesday was swaying and somehow miraculously still on her feet. He approached her at full gallop, reached down and grabbed her by her long, shiny, raven-colored hair, and swung her up behind him on the horse, which naturally knew to do a rollback and sprinted back downhill with two riders on his back now. Somehow, instinctively she wrapped her arms around Joshua and slumped forward against his back, barely conscious.

The detective was proud of Scottie, who had stopped and was providing cover fire as Joshua sped past him, even winking at the teenager as he ran by. The two horses kept down the ridgeline, the Wet Mountain Valley clearly visible and sprawled out below them. Strongheart saw the ridge below was starting to level out among a large jumble of boulders, and he reined up in the rocks.

He quickly dismounted and laid Wednesday down behind a large, house-sized boulder. Scottie followed suit and both men raised their rifles, firing almost simultaneously, and two riders fell off their horses with large spots of blood on their chests.

Joshua looked over at Scottie, who had blood seeping through his arm bandage. Scottie looked back at him and only now saw that Strongheart had been shot through his left hip. Scottie wondered how this amazing man was even walking. The bullet clearly had entered his upper left buttocks and come out low on his left hip, maybe right below the hip bone. The pain, he knew, had to be unbearable.

Scottie yelled, "I'll fire. Bandage your hip!"

Joshua complied, then knelt down by Wednesday, who weakly smiled at him.

She said, "I am dead. You must leave me. I slow you down. I am happy to die with the man I love."

Strongheart said, "Will you shut up?"

"What that means?" she answered weakly.

The shooter gang all dismounted and took cover behind trees. There were now only around a dozen or fewer, and the accurate fire from Joshua and Scottie was unnerving them.

Strongheart was tickled by her saying, *"What that means?"* He started laughing, and she, barely awake, joined in.

Scottie looked over from his boulder and saw them

both laughing, and he started laughing, too. Soon, amid the shooting, all three of them were laughing hysterically, with tears spilling down their cheeks.

Scottie hollered, "I'm hit! You're shot! She is shot to doll rags. Her horse is dead. We are shooting up all our ammunition! Gee, Joshua, thanks for teaching me how to become a Pinkerton. You always get your man!"

This really struck Joshua's funny bone, and he laughed even harder, and Wednesday, seeing this, laughed even harder, too. The gang of bushwhackers heard all the hysterical laughing and howling and were totally frightened now by such bravado in the face of certain death.

The only one not unnerved was the leader of the shooters, dressed in a dapper suit and wearing a derby even in the mountains. It was Bat Masterson. He knew that Joshua Strongheart had been "down the river and over the mountain," as the old frontier cliché went. Joshua had seen it all, and Bat knew he was letting off steam, and so were those with him. He knew that this gang, which he had just joined after riding to the canyon head from the ranch, was after blood but was no match for the Pinkerton.

One of the shooters was a large man named Bullsquat Withers because he always used that term when speaking. Bullsquat looked like a bull himself and was an enormous man of great strength.

He laughed and said, "Wal, boys, I shot thet horse from unner that ole red nigger girl, and ya could see she was bleedin' like a stuck pig already. I think old Strongheart took one, too."

Another man chimed in. "He did! I seen it! He was shot in the ass, and that kid is shot up, too."

Bat looked at the men. "What girl? What kid?"

One of the shooters, a slight, balding man with mean eyes said, "Strongheart has some Injun woman with him, looks like she is a Cheyenne or Sioux, and some kid, a teenaged boy."

Bat Masterson said, "You mean to tell me you men shot a woman?"

Bullsquat said, "She ain't no woman. She is a red blanket nigger. They ain't women. They're animals."

Bat bristled.

He said, "I would love to see you face Joshua Strongheart and say that about her to his face, man to man."

Bullsquat had the gauntlet tossed down now and his manhood called into question. He stood up, towering over Bat Masterson.

The behemoth said, "I ain't afraid ta face him. He's a red nigger, too."

Bat ignored the big man and grabbed his rifle, saying, "I'm going to go parley with Strongheart. You boys hold tight, and don't anybody shoot."

Joshua was changing the dressing on Wednesday's wounds and cleaning them. She was conscious now, having had some water and elk jerky he gave her.

Scottie said, "Joshua, someone's coming with a white truce flag on their rifle barrel."

A voice rang out. "Hello, the boulders!"

Strongheart recognized the voice of Bat Masterson, and he peeked out.

He hollered, "Come on in, Bat!"

Bat Masterson entered the boulders and looked at all three, shaking his head.

"You folks are sure shot up, Strongheart," Bat started, doffing his hat to Wednesday, then saying, "Ma'am, I had no idea you were with Joshua. I do not make war on women or children. Do you speak English, ma'am?"

Strongheart shook hands with Bat, saying, "She does that indeed. This is Wednesday, and she is the daughter of Crazy Horse. She is eaten up with infection, Bat. This is Scottie Middleton, my riding partner."

Scottie's shoulders went back with that remark, and Joshua added, "Wednesday, Scottie, this is my friend Bat Masterson."

Scottie stepped forward, eyes opened wide, and shook hands with Bat, saying, "Please to meet you, sir. You're famous."

Bat and Joshua laughed at this.

Masterson explained, "The ranch foreman said that you and two assassins snuck up over the wall of the ranch and tried to back-shoot V. R. Clinton through the windows with shotguns and rifles."

Strongheart grinned and said, "You have met me and have spoken with me. Do you believe I would do that, Bat?"

Masterson said, "Bullsquat."

Strongheart went on. "Have you met your boss yet?"

Bat said, "No, just a disagreeable ranch foreman."

Strongheart said, "Your boss is not a he, but a she."

Bat said, "What?"

Strongheart said, "V. R. is Victoria Roberta Clinton. She is absolutely beautiful, my friend, but is more deadly than any buzztail you have ever encountered. She was the mistress of Robert Hartwell, whom I killed, the head of the Indian Ring. That's where all the money came from, the misfortunes of my father's people. I had already met her. In fact, she almost killed me in Cañon City. Wiya Waste, we call her Wednesday, rode all the way from the Dakota Territory to warn me about her. She grew up in my father's village."

Bat stuck out his hand, saying, "Your word is gold with me. You need to get her to a hospital somewhere, quick. I ride for the brand, Strongheart."

Joshua said, "I know, Bat. I respect that."

Bat Masterson added, "But the brand has to stand for something decent. I'll hold these boys off as long as I can. Then I know some will come after you. I am sure some will side with me, though, and move on. Most Western men I know won't have anything to do with hurting women, no matter what color their skin is."

Strongheart thanked him and said, "Thanks, Bat. I was going to head to Cañon City down Grape Creek or Copper Gulch Stage Road, but I think we need to go straight to Westcliffe and maybe get a train. I have to get her to Denver to a hospital."

Bat walked Joshua off a few feet and said softly, "When this is all over and you are mended, there is a very disagreeable fellow, a monster actually, named Bullsquat Withers. He found it amusing that she was shot and referred to her and you as *red blanket niggers*. I challenged him to say that face-to-face to you someday, and he said he was not scared to do that."

Joshua shook hands again and gave Bat a knowing look and smile. Scottie shook hands, too.

Bat said, "Wednesday, you could not be in better hands. I know you will get better. I am sorry those men I am with shot you."

She smiled and weakly said, "I know I am in good hands, as you say. I have loved Strongheart since I was a little girl. I like you, Bat."

She smiled and fainted.

Bat said, "Get moving. I'll hold them as long as I can."

Bat left the rocks, pulling his white handkerchief from his barrel. His men were puzzled at seeing Joshua and Scottie mount up, with Joshua holding the limp, wounded woman across his lap on his horse, and head down the mountain at a walk. Nobody in that group, though, would question Bat Masterson, but would wait to hear his words. He walked back to them and called them together. Just in case, he held his right hand on his black-handled, shiny, custom-made .45 revolver with the numeral 1 etched onto the loading gate, just as Bat had designed it.

He said, "Boys, make us a fire. We're camping here tonight."

Bullsquat said, "What about them red niggers? They're getting away!"

Bat got into a gunfighter's crouch and said, "I am the top hand here and give the orders. This outfit is not run by committee. Make camp."

Bullsquat would face any man with his fists, and most with his guns, but not the likes and nerve of Bat Masterson. He turned, grumbling, and set out to gather firewood. Soon a fire was going and coffee was on, and all gathered around the fire, glad to have the shooting over for now.

Joshua held Wednesday in front of him as Eagle, now rested, carefully picked his way down the rocky ridge. Bat had indicated to Strongheart that he would run into a worn wagon road as soon as he left the trees and that he could turn left, go a mile, and turn right again, and Westcliffe would lie before him several miles ahead in the wide open, very green valley.

12

WOUNDS

"Gentlemen," Bat Masterson said, raising his hot cup of coffee in a toast to the gang of sleepy gun hands before him.

It was shortly after dawn the next day, and they were breaking camp.

Bat said, "Boys, I am leaving you all this morning, and although I won't be speaking to him until I get to Cañon City, I am certain I speak for my friend Doc Holliday, too. I found out you boys had shot a woman, and to me, a man who shoots a woman is not a man, but a gelding."

Bullsquat jumped up in anger, but calmed down when he saw Bat's eager smile and his hand hovering over the black-handled, shiny pistol.

Bat said, "Go ahead, Bullsquat. Do you want to join the list?"

Bullsquat slumped and poured himself a cup of coffee.

Bat said, "By the way, boys, V. R. Clinton is a woman, not a man, and she has a bunch of blood money. That's what we were paid with. Any of you want to leave with me, I am heading out."

Three men indicated they were joining him and saddled their horses. Bullsquat and four others were left. One of them was the ranch foreman, Ez Bookman.

Ez said, "Yeah, I knew Miss Clinton was a woman, so she relayed her orders through me on account of she figgered most men wouldn't want no woman ramrod."

Another one said, "I don't care. I ride for the brand."

Bat mounted up and grinned, saying, "You're gonna die for it, too, if you boys try to tangle with Strongheart again."

Bullsquat spit out some tobacco and said, "Bullsquat."

Bat Masterson just laughed, turned his horse, and started down the mountain, his saddle partners following.

Joshua opened his eyes, and it was afternoon, the sun high in the sky to his west. He was dazed and confused, and he slowly started waking, coming to his senses.

There were no mountains around him, and he was in a freight wagon with no top on it. He looked over, and Wednesday lay beside him, asleep. They were lying on mattresses, as far as he could tell, with patchwork quilts on them. She had been rebandaged with good bandages.

Strongheart tried to sit up but could not move. He looked down. His hip and buttocks were bandaged and his leg had completely stiffened up. Grabbing the railing, he pulled hard and raised himself a little. He was in the prairie, and the Greenhorn Mountains were behind him at some distance. He saw a small herd of pronghorns scattering before the wagon and the back of a familiar head of white hair belonging to a slight, older man—it was Zach Banta.

Zach didn't even look at him, but spoke while driving. "Wal, Strongheart, old boy, looks to me like ya saved yer hair again somehow."

Joshua said, "What happened?"

Zach said, "I'll tell ya when ya git up, but you need more rest. Lay back down and close them eyes."

Strongheart felt faint and gladly did as he was told. He was back into a deep sleep almost as soon as he lay back down.

Joshua opened his eyes, and he was lying on the banks of the Arkansas River. The rapids roared past him, and

Belle Ebert stepped out from behind a bush and approached him.

"Belle, you're alive!" he said.

He added, "I thought at first I was dreaming, but this is real. These cliffs rising up above us are real. The river is real. You are real. Am I in Heaven? Can I kiss you?"

She smiled broadly, looking more beautiful than she had ever been, and she said, "Please do. I have missed you so much, my darling."

They kissed, long and passionately.

They pulled apart, and he just smiled at her and pulled her to him.

He said, "I am confused. I love this, but I'm confused. You were murdered. You were raped and murdered, but now you are whole. Belle, you have never looked more beautiful. Am I dreaming?"

She said, "No, Joshua. You are here with me now. This is real, and I love you, darling. I always will."

"I love you, too, and I have missed you so much—so very much," he said.

She twisted her head to the side and laid it on her left hand, which was on top of a boulder.

Strongheart said, "'See, how she leans her cheek upon her hand! O, that I were a glove upon that hand, that I might touch that cheek!'"

Belle said, "Shakespeare again. *Romeo and Juliet*, Act II. See, I'm onto you now, Joshua."

He said, "How did you know that was from *Romeo and Juliet*?"

She said, "There is much that I know now that I never knew before. I know many things, my love."

He said, "I know that I will never stop loving you, Belle."

She said, "As it should be. But your heart is troubled, Joshua. You want to love others, or another, but you are worried that you will not be loyal to me."

Belle continued, "Shakespeare also said, 'Love sought is good, but given unsought is better.'"

Joshua said, "I don't understand."

She said, "Yes, you do. Shakespeare also said, 'Go to your bosom; Knock there, and ask your heart what it doth know.' Joshua, do you believe God put love in your heart for me?"

"Yes. Yes, I do," he said.

She replied, "God puts all love in your heart. If He puts love for another in your heart, who are you to deny it?"

Strongheart had a lump in his throat and said, "What about you, Belle?"

She said, "You asked me if you are in Heaven. No, a little bit of Heaven is in you. It is in your heart, and I am in your heart and will always dwell there. I am very happy and safe now. You have much to give, and it is only right that you give it to another. You survive. That is what you do, and you save others. That is to you what breathing is to other men. Keep saving and keep loving, Joshua Strongheart. I will always be here for you, in your heart to call upon when you need me. Follow your heart. Your mind will lead you astray."

He opened his eyes and blinked them. The sun was low in the western sky, hovering over the Greenhorn Mountains, far behind them now. Strongheart shook his head. His dream had been so real. It seemed like he was not dreaming. Moaning, he pulled himself into a sitting position and looked around. Wednesday was still sleeping. He touched her cheek, and it felt warm.

Zach looked back over his shoulder, saying, "Wal, Joshua, guess ya had yoreself a nice little nap, did ya?"

Strongheart said, "I was just dreaming—a very realistic dream. I even asked during the dream if I was dreaming."

Zach said, "Reckon so. Ya was talkin' ta Belle. Ya talked in yore sleep. Mentioned her name."

"I talked in my sleep?" Strongheart said. "I never talk in my sleep. I cannot afford to. Might happen when I am sleeping close to an enemy."

Zach replied, "Reckon so. I take it as a compliment. Ya woke up, knew ya was with me, and fell back asleep knowing ya was safe."

Joshua said, "Makes sense. You have different horses. What happened?"

Zach chuckled, cracked the whip, and said, "Get up there, boys!"

Strongheart watched the horses break into a trot and could see the tops of some buildings in Pueblo in the distance.

Zach said, "I had them unhitch mah team and hitch up these stagecoach hosses thet was lent by the Wells Fargo boys. Ain't that nice?"

Joshua smiled, and Zach continued, "Wal, I reckon you come waltzin' into Westcliffe carryin' this young lady in yore arms, barely able ta walk. Thet Scottie boy was ridin' his big black and leadin' Eagle fer ya. Eagle had thrown a shoe and had worn his hoof down to the frog jest about. All heart, thet horse is. You wouldn't let thet horse carry ya one more mile, and ya walked carryin' her fer several miles. The doctor treated all three of ya and said she had to get to the hospital quick. They was gonna send you down ta Cañon City by rail, then to Pueblo, then ta Denver."

He chuckled and continued, "I said, 'Gimme some faster horses and I'll get him ta Pueblo quicker than any old trains can. It's a straight shot, boys.' They fetched me this team, doctor treated ya, and here we are."

"Thanks, old-timer," Joshua said. "Where is Scottie? Where is Eagle?"

Zach responded, "Reckon he is on his way down Grape Creek on the Rio Grande Line ta Cañon City. Bat Masterson come down outta the mountains and tole

217

what happened. Said he would see Scottie ta home, and they'd make sure Eagle got stabled and fixed up with the blacksmith. Blacksmith here said he figgered Eagle would need ta rest his legs a bit and let thet hoof heal a few days before he got new shoes. He put some salve on it he swears by."

"What about Scottie's wound?"

Zach said, "Aw, it weren't no more 'n a scratch. Doc patched him up and said he'll have hisself a good ole scar for the womenfolk to carry on over. Tell you what, Strongheart, thet young man has some bottom to him."

Strongheart grinned and thought about how proud he was of the man Scottie was becoming.

Joshua moved forward and sat down next to Zach.

Zach said, "Yer rifle, bedroll, and saddlebags are in the back there, and here's yer rig."

He reached under the buckboard bench and pulled out Joshua's gun belt with his pistol and large knife. Joshua nodded in appreciation and put them on. He tried to stretch his leg out. He had never had his hip hurt so badly.

"I tole Bat Masterson who yer boss is, and he is sending him a telegraph when he gets ta Cañon City," Zach said. "He also said ta tell ya not ta worry about thet Scottie boy, as he and Doc Holliday will keep an eye on him whilst they're in town."

"Boy, oh, boy," Strongheart said. "Zach, I can't tell you how much I appreciate your friendship, and it looks like I made some good friends in Bat and Doc, too."

Zach said, "Young man, reckon ya really don't know how many people ya got coverin' yer back door. I ever tell ya of the ole boy who had friends watchin' out fer him?"

Joshua laughed and said, "No, but I suspect you will."

Zach said, "There was this ole boy that had run outta luck and had a posse of fifteen chasin' him. You know the Mogollon Rim country down New Mexico way?"

Strongheart said, "Yes, sir."

Zach went on, "Well, this ole boy was holed up there down at the Mogollon Rim with his gang. From what I understan', this ole boy and his amigos went into a bank down there near the border and took upon themselves ta make a large bank withdrawal. That woulda been okay, 'ceptin' they didn't have no deposit or funds sittin' in the bank at the time, only a strong desire to make a quick withdrawal. Wal, they reckoned they could do it quicker by drawin' their hoglegs and wearin' kerchiefs over their faces in case too much dust was stirred up by the eagerness of them bank employees to oblige their request."

Joshua, despite his pain, was laughing already, and they were now riding into the western outskirts of Pueblo.

Zach continued, "So this posse formed that was not appreciative of this ole boy's banking practices. They come out to give him and his gang their comeuppance. So, after some lead flying back and forth, he stuck out a flag of truce. He told his gang to cover his backside fer him whilst he tried to parley with the lawmen. He goes walking out with that flag, which happened to make a good target, and the next thing ya know, the marshal grabs iron and opens up the ball. This ole boy was shot ta doll rags, and crawled back to his gang, near dead. He said, 'You boys tole me ya was coverin' my backside fer me. What the hell happened?'

"One a them outlaws said, 'We did, boss. All a them bullet holes are in yer front. Ya ain't got a single hole in yore backside.'"

Strongheart chuckled, then laughed hard.

He said, "Zach, you sure have a way with a story."

Banta grinned at him.

An hour later, the wagon pulled up to the Pueblo train depot, and two Pinkerton agents appeared out of the crowd. Strongheart knew them both.

They shook with Joshua, who introduced them to Zach Banta.

Jules Carter said, "We've been down here a week. Lucky sent us down to investigate V. R. Clinton for you, and we weren't able to come up with much. Then we heard from Lucky that V. R. stands for Victoria Roberta Clinton."

Strongheart said, "Yes, and she is a looker who will steal your heart as easy as you please. Of course, while she is doing that, she will reach back and steal your wallet, your pocket watch, the watch fob, and the jingle-bobs off your spurs if they are made of anything other than steel."

The men chuckled.

Jules said, "We have orders from Chicago and have a nurse. She just went to get coffee and will accompany you and your lady friend to the hospital in Denver. The company hired her to be your personal nurse. Boy, I never saw an Injun that beautiful before. Come to think of it, Strongheart, that has to be about the most beautiful face I have ever seen on any woman."

Joshua responded, "Her Lakota name is Wiya Waste. It means 'beautiful woman.' I call her Wednesday. That name will make it easier for her dealing with white people."

Jules said, "The hospital in Denver is expecting you both, and they have people ready to operate on her right away. I guess one person gave Lucky some guff about Wednesday here being an Injun, and he telegraphed some doctor that took care of him before."

Strongheart laughed, thinking about when Lucky was lingering near death in the same hospital. He'd had a good doctor, because Joshua had had him before, too.

Jules went on, "I guess this doctor lit into that woman like a marmot after a prairie dog and tore her hide into several shreds. She's looking for a new job somewhere besides Denver, I'll bet."

Strongheart knew that Jules was going to tell him she was fired. Wednesday's concerns, and his little concern about her being treated poorly, proved to be unnecessary. He sure appreciated his boss and realized again how fortunate he was to have so many friends.

On the train, able again to relax, he fell asleep in the private car reserved for Wednesday and him by Allan Pinkerton himself. Joshua was so tired by the time they were loaded on the train, he did not even hear the name of the nurse, which was Teresa Williams—a very nice, caring person with blond hair and a pleasant smile. He did remember that.

The Union Pacific Railway Hospital was located near York Street and Fortieth Avenue in Denver, Colorado. A two-and-a-half-story, rusticated stone structure with dormers, it had nine chimneys that Joshua had counted the last time he was there. He and Wednesday were brought there by ambulance after the train arrived at Union Pacific Station downtown.

Joshua was taken into the hospital in a wooden wheelchair, and he saw Wednesday being carried in on a stretcher. Nurses and doctors were scurrying in and out of doorways, and Joshua got up slowly out of his chair and started down the hallway. He spotted a doctor behind a desk and hobbled into his office.

The doctor, a gray-haired, distinguished-looking man with a well-trimmed beard, did not even greet him but instead hollered, "Nurse! A chair!"

Seconds later, a nurse appeared in the doorway pushing another wooden wheelchair, and the doctor said, "Sit down," not "Would you please sit down?" or anything close, but a firm command.

Joshua collapsed into the chair and said, "Doctor, the young lady, the Lakota woman who was brought in just now—I need to speak to her doctor."

The doctor said, "That is me. I am Thaddeus Wintergarden, and I know who you are, Mr. Strongheart. What is her name?"

Strongheart said, "Wednesday."

The stern-looking doctor smiled.

He said, "Now there is a name. I like that."

Joshua said, "Thank you, Doctor."

"You mean to tell me you named her that?"

Strongheart said, "Yes, the other day. Her Lakota name—Lakota is what you white men call the Sioux—is Wiya Waste, which means 'beautiful woman.' I called her Wednesday because it sounds close."

"Very clever," the doctor said. "Well, my goal will be to call her Healthy Woman when she leaves here, instead of Beautiful Woman. Now, what is your question?"

Joshua smiled broadly and said, "You've already answered the question, Doctor."

"No more getting out of chairs when you are placed in them, Mr. Strongheart."

Strongheart said, "Call me Joshua, please. I will be a good patient. Just take good care of her."

The doctor said, "We will be operating on her shortly. Probably will operate on you right after. A nurse will take you to your room, and I will be in to see you soon. Take a nap while you wait."

Strongheart was not used to be being bossed around, but saw that this man was accustomed to giving orders and having them obeyed. He would cooperate fully, as he respected the doctor.

He opened his eyes and looked around. It was night outside, and his eyes closed again while he slipped back into a deep, comfortable sleep.

The next time Joshua opened his eyes, it was daytime. He stretched, and Dr. Wintergarden walked in the door.

His stern look changed to a pleasant smile, and he said, "Good morning, Joshua. How are you feeling today?"

Strongheart said, "Honestly, Doctor, I am hoping this is the last time I ever spend a night at this hospital."

The doctor grinned and replied, "A night? You arrived here three days ago."

Joshua was shocked to hear he had been there three days.

The doctor continued, "I was told you carried Wednesday in your arms for several miles. You were shot through your hip and had part of your hip bone nicked away, and a sliver of bullet was lodged in the injured hip bone. How were you able to overcome the pain you must have been in?"

Strongheart said, "I didn't do anything, Dr. Wintergarden, but how is Wednesday?"

The stern look returned. "Not good, I'm afraid. She has had a serious infection and lost a lot of blood, which has left her weak. I think we have the infection healing. I had to make a few incisions to let her bleed out some of the infection and have used a honey salve. You did an excellent job on her wound, and the bullet passed cleanly through, it seems."

Joshua said, "Then what is wrong?"

The doctor said, "It is touch and go. I just don't know. She has a strep infection, but I think it is subsiding. Her fever is gone, but she is weak and cannot even sit up yet. She has been awake several times, but it is almost like she has lost the will to live. I wish I knew how to snap her out of it."

Strongheart said, "Can I see her?"

The physician said, "Of course. Her room is next door, and the nurse just told me she has been opening her eyes a bit. Hold on."

He walked to a closet in the corner, opened the oak door, and pulled out a pair of crude wooden crutches, which were actually two long sticks with padded handles to go under the armpits. The bottom of each crutch had a tight leather boot stitched around it.

Strongheart walked over to a window in the hallway and looked out at the mountains. He wished desperately to be there right now—anywhere but here. He thought about his mother's death and how close he had been with her. She was only fifteen when he was born, but she never acted like a girl. She was always a strict, loving mother who would not baby him and made sure he got plenty of education, and she left him early. He remembered visiting her in the hospital and begging her not to give up, not to give in to the consumption, but the disease was too much for her. It actually made him feel worse that she had left him a very large estate. Joshua Strongheart was rich, but he had his money in banks and investments and had sought out a career, and he loved the work he chose with the Pinkerton Agency. Strongheart looked out at the mountain range west of Denver and the snowcapped peaks. He said a silent prayer and asked God to give him the right words to save this woman's life.

He limped into the room of Wiya Waste. He smiled as he looked around. She was used to living in a bison-hide teepee, and here she was in a room that looked like it had been a doctor's office that was converted into a patient's private room. It had fancy wallpaper on the walls, and sheer drapes, valances, and curtains on the windows. He appreciated the treatment she was being afforded.

Strongheart pulled a chair over to her bedside and leaned his crutches against her bed as he sat down stiffly in the straight-backed chair. A nurse was in the room, but he waited until she finished placing bandaging, iodine, and the like. The beautiful Wednesday lay there on her side, curled up in the fetal position. He touched her, and for the first time since she had been shot, she did not feel warm to the touch. Her color was better, but she looked like she was ready to die. The nurse left.

Joshua said, *"Wiya Waste. Wiya Waste, hau. Tókheškhe yaúŋ he?"* Which means "Beautiful Woman, Beautiful Woman, hello. How are you?"

Her eyelids flickered, but she kept her head on her pillow and looked at him and closed her eyes again.

He moaned and said, *"Tóhaŋni waŋžíla iyápi iyóhi šni yeló,"* which means, "One language is never enough."

He said, "Please open your eyes. I have to tell you something very, very important."

Inside her brain, she secretly felt that he was about to tell her on behalf of the doctor that she was going to die, and he was going to tell her good-bye. She also did not want to open her eyes, as it felt so good to just rest and not fight anymore. This was all so foreign to her, and the infection made her feel so bad. She had seen so many Lakota die of infections over the years, and she was so weak and sick when she came in that she just assumed she was going to make the journey.

With her voice very weak, she spoke slowly, saying, *"Hau, Wanji Wambli, híŋhaŋni lahči,"* which meant, "Hello, One Eagle, good morning."

Strongheart said, "Can you keep your eyes open and look at me, so I know you are hearing every word I say?"

The beauty said, weakly again, "Yes."

She kept her eyes open readily, since looking at this man with love in her eyes had been her favorite thing to do since she was four or five years old. He was her hero then and had remained so her whole life. In fact, her love for him had grown over the years more rapidly than her age advanced.

Strongheart said, "Have you not told me many times that you love me?"

Her eyes opened wider and her voice was a little stronger as she said, "Yes, yes, *Iyótaŋčhila,* Joshua!" Which means, "Yes, yes, I love you, Joshua!"

"Do you love me a lot?"

She wondered why he was saying this, but responded with an even stronger voice, "Yes, I love you very, very much. Why?"

Strongheart looked at the wall, then back at her, saying, "I want to ask you to do something for me because you love me. You probably will not want to do it, but I am asking you to do it for me. Will you do whatever I ask, because it is for me?"

Wednesday said, "Yes, yes, I will."

He said, "Good. You may not understand all my words, but you will get the meaning. I want you to get your pretty red diseased ass out of this bed and Lakota the hell up!!!"

This totally caught her by surprise, made her angry, and gave her hope all at once, since she had been expecting him to say good-bye, as she was going to make the journey.

Wednesday said, "Yes, I will," and she put her hands down, and with her arms shaking, she pushed herself off the bed.

She was breathing hard, but very proud of herself, and he was proud of her, too. He wrapped his arms around her and hugged her.

She smiled and seemed much more alive.

She said, "I thought you would tell me good-bye, that I must make the walk."

He laughed and said, "Heck no. You never heard me say a curse word before, did you?"

"What does *curse word* mean?"

He laughed again. "Bad words for Americans."

She said, "Oh, no, I had not. You, a what does it mean, you shock me."

She giggled.

He said, "How about some food?"

She said, "Yes, my stomach thinks a wolf lives inside it."

Strongheart said, "Nurse!"

Teresa, who had been welcomed by the hospital, came in from the hallway and smiled at Wednesday.

She said, "Hi, Wednesday, do you remember me?"

Wednesday said, "Yes, you are Teresa. You help me. Thank you."

Teresa said, "I am glad to see you have decided to live. How about some nice beef stew?"

Wednesday smiled and gave her a quizzical look.

Strongheart said, "That is soup with beef from cows, carrots, potatoes, and onions all in gravy."

"That sounds like very good. Thank you."

Wednesday was not used to saying thank you in her

society, as it was usually understood, but was learning the white man's ways rapidly.

Strongheart said, "I'm going to let you eat. I want you to get stronger. It is a long way back to the Dakota Territory, and a hard journey."

She said, "What about Victoria?"

He said, "Right now, I just want you to worry about getting better."

She said, "Wanji Wambli, she was part of killing many of our people. I want to be there when you put chains on her and she goes to jail."

He said, "Heal fast, and we will talk about it."

He went to his room and lay down, as he was feeling a little weak. Joshua was very excited about the way Wednesday had responded to him. He drifted off to sleep. An hour passed, and Strongheart felt a presence. He opened his eyes, and there in the doorway was Brenna Alexander. She came to his bedside, bent down, and kissed him.

"Brenna," he said, "what are you doing here?"

She said, "I ran into Lucky Champ in a restaurant in downtown Chicago, and he told me what happened to you and where you were. I booked a ride on the next train here. How are you feeling?"

When she walked over and kissed him, she and Joshua did not see Wednesday being wheeled into his room in a wooden wheelchair by Teresa. The nurse quickly backed out of the door and wheeled Wednesday back to her room. The Lakota woman could hardly contain her tears until the nurse wisely left the room and closed the door.

Strongheart got out of bed and grabbed his crutches. His pain was terrible as the pair walked out the door and down the hallway. She told Joshua what had been happening in her life. He felt strange talking to her, even getting a kiss from her, because of Wednesday being in the next room and professing her love for him so freely. They walked to the end of the hallway and turned down another one and ended up at a window facing the cityscape of downtown Denver, which was actually blocks away.

Brenna said, "I missed you so much and have been so worried about you since I heard. I cried most of the way to Denver on the train."

For some reason this statement bothered Joshua. Why did she tell him that? he wondered.

She moved up close to him again, wanting to be kissed. He stopped and looked out the window. Brenna turned him toward her.

She said, "I love you, Joshua."

He did not know how to respond. He pulled her close in a hug. Strongheart was very confused right now about women. After his realistic dream, he really felt the final bit of healing after losing Belle. He would always love her and have a special place in his heart for her, but he felt she somehow, from Heaven, had told him it was okay to love again. He knew Wiya Waste grew up in the lodges of the Lakota, and it was not even fair to ask her to live in the white man's world.

Just now, his long-held fantasies about her were coming to the fore, since he had learned after all these years that they were not actually cousins. They were unrelated as far as blood goes. He was also very impressed that she was actually the daughter of Crazy Horse. He did think, *What a family of warriors we could breed and raise!*

Brenna said, "Joshua, do you love me?"

He smiled softly and said, "Do I love you, or am I in love with you?"

She said, "Yes, are you in love with me?"

He said, "Brenna, this is crazy, but right now I am not sure about anything or anybody. I do love you, but I do not know if I am in love with you. You are beautiful, and you are really a wonderful lady. I just don't know."

She smiled and walked slowly down the hallway and around the corner.

Joshua felt bad for her and did not know how he should have answered her. He knew he was not ever going to see her again. They had been through a lot together, but she now lived the life of a wealthy woman in Chicago. He had to concentrate on getting better and stronger. He still had unfinished business with Victoria Clinton and her gunmen.

Joshua visited with Wednesday most of the next day, and she seemed like she was normal except for still needing to gain strength. She seemed somewhat withdrawn from him. He did not understand, but he also grinned, knowing he would never understand women.

The next day, they ate together, and they spoke.

Strongheart said, "It is hard for you among the *wasicun*?"

"No," she said. "It is easy. I am learning to speak American. I mean English. And learning many things about the *wasicun*."

He said, "The past two days you have been different, like you are far away. What troubles your heart?"

The beauty replied, "Who was that pretty woman who came to see you?"

"Oh," he said, realizing she must have seen them in the hallway, or maybe had even seen her kissing him.

He said, "Her name is Brenna, and she lives very far away in a city like this one called Chicago."

Wednesday said, "On the big lake."

He said, "You are learning a lot.

"She is my friend," he said. "She came to see me because she heard I was hurt."

Wednesday said, "Zach is your friend, but I did not see you kiss him."

Strongheart chuckled, and his face reddened.

He said, "She is my close friend. She has counted coup with me. She is a good woman."

"Is she your woman?"

"No, she is not," he said. "She loves me, but I am not in love with her. I am very confused right now."

Wednesday was very relieved when she heard his answer.

She said, "Your heart is not thinking about love right now. Your heart only thinks about Victoria and her bad men. You should just think of that right now, and your heart will tell you when it wants to talk of love."

He grinned, and then chuckled. She was right.

Two days later, Lucky appeared at Joshua's door and soon met Wednesday. Strongheart told him the story about them being cousins for so many years and then finding out that she was actually not related to him and was the daughter of Crazy Horse.

Lucky said, "Young lady, do you realize how fortunate you are?"

Wednesday liked this man.

"What do you mean, *fortunate*?" she asked.

"How lucky you are. . . . How honored you are," he responded.

She turned to Joshua for help, saying, *"Owákahniğe šni,"* which meant, "I don't understand."

The handsome half-breed smiled and said, "You are like a queen because you are the daughter of Crazy Horse. Do you understand?"

"Yes, but he is the enemy of the *wasicun*?" she said.

Lucky commented, "But he is famous. He was a hero . . . a mighty warrior of your people. Not all white men hate the Indians."

She smiled and said, "Not all red people hate the white people."

Later, Strongheart and Lucky walked outside the hospital and talked.

Lucky said, "Joshua, Allan Pinkerton despised Robert Hartwell, too. This woman, this Victoria Clinton, is the devil's mistress. He wants you to bring her castle down around her ears."

Strongheart said, "Happily. But I can't leave Wednesday alone here in the hospital. I have been waiting for her to get the strength to travel, then I'll send her home."

Lucky chuckled. "*Mon ami*, my friend, do you think I am blind?"

Strongheart said, "Yeah, I have feelings for her, boss, but she grew up in a lodge tanning hides, gathering firewood, hunting, and so on. I am not going to spend my days in a teepee, and I could never ask her to live in a house like a white man."

Lucky said, "*Sacre bleu!* Joshua, don't you think that should be her decision? You mentioned she hunts. Didn't you teach her how to be a good hunter?"

"I thought she was my first cousin then, alone without a man," Joshua said. "I told her to hold out until the right man came along and that she had to survive until then."

Lucky laughed and lit a cigar.

He said, "*Monsieur* Strongheart, if you taught her to hunt and such things, could you not teach her how to live in our society?"

Strongheart looked off at the distant peaks, saying, "I suppose. Lucky, why are you trying to push me into a relationship with Wednesday?"

Lucky said, "Because I know you better than any-body. I see how you look at her, and how she looks at you. Most men would keel to have a woman love them so strongly, my friend."

Strongheart said, "She should be plenty strong in a few days, and I will send her home, and then head back myself to get Clinton and her gang."

Lucky said, "She came all those miles to you to warn you about her and tell you who she was. She did that in a white man's world. She told me that she wants to be there with you when you go after Clinton. I think your father's people, by what she told me, want her there with you to see this through."

Strongheart said, "It is pretty amazing that she traveled so far in a white man's world to find me. I never even took the time since then to think on it. How did she do it?"

"She and her horse traveled by boxcars and stock cars," Lucky said. "You still think thees woman could not live in a white man's world?"

Strongheart said, "She is pretty amazing."

13

THE FINISH

It was a week later that a much-rested Joshua Strong-heart and a much healthier Wednesday boarded the train at Union Station to make the journey back to Pueblo, then to Cañon City. Strongheart picked up Eagle the next day at the blacksmith's. His hoof had healed, and he was wearing four new shoes and seemed excited to see his master and buddy, Joshua. The blacksmith, who also ran the livery stable on Main Street in Cañon City, had a well-broke Appaloosa gelding named Pebbles that had been owned by a local rancher who had died in a flash flood. Joshua had met the man one time, and he was quite a character.

Strongheart had asked the man, who was named Adamic, one time why he rode an Appy when so many cowboys frowned on them and said they were only fit for Indians. Adamic took a big bite out of his plug of tobacco, chewed on it a few minutes, then looked at the Pinkerton and replied, "Son, this here country is nasty, nasty. There's a bunch a rocks around these parts that like ta move from time to time, and when they do, I want me a horse that don't. A good Appaloosa can go and go all day, like an Arabian, and they are fit and bred fer the mountains. This here is a mountain horse."

Then grinning, he added, "Mah horse might be ugly, but he's stupid."

Pebbles was well muscled and beautiful. He was called a leopard Appaloosa, which meant he had white over his body, covered by evenly spaced sorrel, or red, spots all over, looking somewhat like a leopard in his overall appearance. He had a white mane and tail and black-and-white hooves, which were loved by black-smiths, as they had both hardness and give to them. They lasted much longer than white hooves and did not crack as easily as brittle solid black hooves.

Scottie rode into Cañon City and found Strongheart and Wiya Waste riding along the Arkansas River.

Joshua said, "Come on, Scottie. I'm buying you two a great dinner."

He led them to the French Restaurant, and they entered. The same waitress smiled broadly when she saw them, but then her smile turned to a frown as she looked at Wednesday.

Strongheart said, *"Bonjour, mademoiselle. Comment-allez vous?"*

She replied, *"Bonjour, Monsieur Strongheart. Je vais bien, merci. Et vous?"*

He said, "I'm fine, but why did you make the face? Do you have a problem with us being here?"

"Non, monsieur," she said, red-faced. "I do not, but—but thees ees the headquarters for the Ku Klux Klan in the territory, and . . ."

Strongheart put his hand up, smiling, and said, "The hell with the Klan. If they have a problem with the company I keep or me, send them to me."

She laughed at this prospect, saying, *"Oui, monsieur.* Please be seated where you would like."

Joshua led them to a table in the corner, and he sat facing the door.

She handed each a menu and said, "Drinks?"

Strongheart said, "Do you have iced tea? We do not want any liquor today, thank you."

She said, *"Oui, monsieur."*

He said, "Iced tea for each of us, with sugar."

Wednesday said, "Iced tea?"

Scottie said, "You're going to love it, Wednesday."

It was soon placed before them, and she did.

The two let Joshua order for them, so after hors d'oeuvres he ordered. For himself, *lamb noisette*, a fennel and lavender roasted rack of lamb with a sweet-bread and roasted-shallot stuffing with plum tomato and olive tapenade.

Then, for Wednesday, he ordered *filet mignon à la Bordelaise*, which was grilled medallions of beef tenderloin sautéed in Chablis, shallots, thyme, lemon, and veal glacé, with potato gratin, and topped with mushrooms.

Scottie had *poulet chasseur*, made with braised chicken, roasted beets with beet greens, garlic chive mashed potatoes, and tomato-flavored demi-glace.

Wednesday looked at him and, eyes opened wide, said, "Do the *wasicun* eat like this all the time?"

Joshua and Scottie both got a very big chuckle out of this.

Strongheart said, "No, this is a very expensive restaurant with fine foods from France. I will show you a globe and explain where it is, where we are, and where Denver and your home are. I thought you might like a nice meal. Tomorrow we will be up in Westcliffe, and we might not eat well like this for a while.

"Scottie," Strongheart said over hot coffee some time later, "how is your arm?"

Scottie said, "It's fine. Just a new scar now. Joshua, while you were gone, I made a very important decision. I think it was because of what we went through up there and things I have seen since I have been with you."

"What's that, Scottie?" Joshua said, curious.

Scottie smiled. "Well, sir, I am not going to become

a Pinkerton." His face reddened, and he continued, "I have seen things like what we just saw when we first came in. There is so much hate and anger all the time. I have seen how people sometimes treat you and now Wednesday because of skin color. I had all that hatred in my home with my drunken uncle, and even in the way my folks died. Instead of sending bad people to hell like you do, Joshua, I want to catch them early and try to direct them toward Heaven. I'm going to get my education like you and my aunt have told me to do over and over, and I am going to become a sky pilot."

"You're going to become a preacher!" Joshua said. "That is wonderful, Scottie!"

Strongheart shook hands with him and then directed his attention to Wednesday to explain, "He will become a medicine man like Sitting Bull is."

She leaned forward and said, "Scottie, that is a very good thing. With my people, that is much better than to be a chief. Being a medicine man is the same as number one, instead of number three or four."

Strongheart shook his head, smiling. In Denver, she had started to learn about numbers from Teresa and was now using the number one to place a top value on being a medicine man. With the Lakota, medicine was faith and spirituality, not actual medicine. The Pinkerton was impressed that she assigned the number to show how important the position was.

Scottie beamed.

Strongheart said, "Scottie, when it is time for you to

start college, you let me know, and I am going to pay for it, all the way until you become a preacher."

Scottie was very moved and could hardly speak to explain it.

He nodded and meekly mumbled, "Thank you, sir. God bless you."

They left the restaurant, and Joshua took Wednesday to his small ranch south of town, and she was very impressed. Unlike the arid soil all around the area, the soil at the ranch was very good because of its proximity to the Arkansas River, which flowed—or, actually, roared—through town. She started cleaning and placing items in more efficient spots.

Strongheart grinned and said, "Nest builder."

The next morning, they loaded their horses into a freight car on the narrow-gauge railroad that ran up Grape Creek, and they were in Westcliffe well before noon. As always, Zach Banta had gotten word ahead of time about Joshua's return, so he had already gone to Westcliffe with his buckboard to get supplies.

The three had lunch together, and Zach said, "Reckon she has that big old Bullsquat with her now, and three others. Thet new foreman a hers was at a saloon down ta Cañon City, McClure's, the other night and was drinkin' and tryin' ta show off his new Colt Russian .44 and tripped over a chair leg and accidental-like put a bullet right through his own beer mug. Problem was, he was a holdin' it up to his lips at the time. It taken the top a his head clean off. The real cowboys she had decided they din't need no severance pay. They jest took her herd instead. Heerd they was pushin' it toward Kansas. Now ya only have to deal with four coon-dogs and one hellcat. They are holed up in her ranch. Deputies, nobody has been able ta git in."

Joshua said firmly, "I will."

Zach smiled and said, "'Spect so."

Strongheart said, "I have to stop at the mercantile. Wednesday, I would like you to stay here with Zach until I return. If that is okay with you, Zach?"

Wednesday started to speak, but Strongheart gave her that look that clearly showed this was not up for debate.

Zach said, "Okay with me. Look how purty thet little thing is, and how ugly and old I am. Ya think I mind one bit, yer crazy."

Joshua got ready to saddle up to leave, and Wednesday jumped forward and confronted him.

"Joshua," she said, "be careful."

One thing she had learned to do was kiss as good as any white woman, and she did so now. He smiled down at her and mounted up. He would ride west, then would stop at the mercantile briefly, then turn south.

Two hours later, he rode through the front gate of Victoria Clinton's ranch, but the place looked bare except for a large herd of antelope out in the lush green pasture. In a few hours, it would be invaded by a large harem of elk and, at the other end, a large herd of mule deer.

He rode up to the front gate, knowing they were all hunkered down inside. He then skirted the big stone wall and grabbed bundles of dynamite from his saddlebags, lit the fuses, and dropped them at several spots around the wall. Then, returning to the front gate, he dropped two bundles there after lighting them, and he ran his horse back. Joshua waited a few minutes.

The gate exploded into numerous splinters of oak and shards of brass and, less than two minutes later, three separate explosions blew giant sections of the rock wall inward, shattering windows and crashing holes in the big ranch house in several places.

Bullsquat and the three gunmen got behind windows in the living room, their rifles poised and ready to shoot. They heard thundering hooves approaching and tensed up, aiming at the opening where the gate had been. Suddenly, Eagle ran through the gate, but he was carrying nothing but Joshua's saddle.

At the same time, Strongheart ran through the western hole in the stone wall and tossed his last dynamite package into the middle of the house, this time with a short fuse. He ran quickly outside and ducked behind the damaged wall, and it exploded within seconds. The rest of the home's windows blew outward, and the three gunmen came out the door gasping and choking on smoke and dust.

They looked all around, guns ready, and finally spun around when they heard Strongheart say, "Boys, up here."

They saw him standing on the small porch on the second floor, and he drew quickly and fired, fanning his gun, and bullet holes appeared in the chest of each killer, except Bullsquat, whose carbine stock exploded from the bullet's impact. He was staring at Joshua Strongheart, who was thumbing new shells into his Peacemaker. Joshua jumped down on the ground, facing Bullsquat at fifteen paces.

Bullsquat grinned evilly and rolled up his sleeves, fully exposing the ham-sized fists and tree-trunk forearms.

He said, "All right, Strongheart, Ah've seen ya shoot. Now let's see how ya are with them fists. Ah can take you any day."

Joshua said, "We'll never know. You're heeled. Draw!"

Panic opened Bullsquat's eyes and he said, "I'm gonna kill you!"

Joshua said, "Bullsquat!"

The big man clawed for his gun and looked into the barrel of Strongheart's Peacemaker, wondering how he got it out so fast. He saw flames shoot out twice and looked down at his chest, which was now covered in blood. He couldn't breathe, and he panicked even more and started clawing at his shirt.

Strongheart spun around, sensing a presence behind

him, and Victoria Clinton stood there in a sheer negligee. She apparently was ready to use her own weapon.

She said, "Joshua, I'm not going to prison. You are too much of a gentleman to shoot me. I am rich—very rich—and all this can be yours."

He said, "On the dead bodies of American Indian men, women, and children. I don't think so, woman. You're going to prison for the rest of your life."

She pulled a derringer out, pointing it at him, and said, "No, I'm not going to prison. You could have had me. But you turned it down. Now you're going to die, and I will be in New Mexico by nightfall, drinking brandy."

A voice behind him made him spin around, and there was Wednesday, standing where the gate had been, her bow in her hand with an arrow drawn.

She said, "No, you will not kill him. You will die, and you know how pretty you are? My arrow goes into your pretty face, because of what you and your man did to my people. You die now."

Victoria panicked and felt faint from sheer terror.

With that, Wiya Waste released the arrow, and it sliced right past Joshua's ear. He turned his head and saw it penetrate Victoria's forehead and exit the back of her skull, killing her instantly. She fell forward into the dirt, her face a bloody mess.

Joshua turned, and Wednesday ran forward, dropping her bow, and threw herself into his arms, kissing him passionately.

He smiled, looked into her tear-filled eyes, and said, "I thought I told you to stay with Zach. Wednesday Strongheart, if I am going to be your husband, you need to start listening to me."

A stone fell off the crumbling wall, the first of many in the years to come. Eagle and Pebbles whinnied softly to each other, and several birds in the trees outside the wall chirped. A bald eagle flew high overhead, circling in the valley winds.

ABOUT THE AUTHOR

Don Bendell is a bestselling author whose style has been likened to that of Louis L'Amour and Zane Grey. He is a 100 percent disabled Green Beret Vietnam veteran and a 1995 inductee into the International Karate and Kickboxing Hall of Fame. Don's late wife of thirty-three years, Shirley, and he were the only couple in history to both be inducted into the Hall of Fame. Don owns the Strongheart Ranch in southern Colorado, named for his number one bestselling western, its sequel *Blood Feather* (Berkley/Penguin Random House, August 2013), and the sequels *The Indian Ring* (Berkley/Penguin Random House, January 2016) and *The Rider of Phantom Canyon* (Berkley/Penguin Random House, October 2016). There are over three million copies of his twenty-eight books in print. Don hit number one on Amazon three times and was nominated for the Pulitzer Prize for one of his books, *Tracks of Hope: A Modern Day Western* (2011, GoldMinds Publishing, Nashville). He has a master's degree in business leadership from Grand Canyon University and has six grown children and eleven grandchildren, and is a widower after losing his wife/best friend/soul mate, Shirley, to the side effects of a stem cell transplant after conquering leukemia with blast crisis. She passed away on Valentine's Day 2014 with Don at her side. Don has horses, alpacas, blue-green and white peacocks, chickens, dogs, and cats, and enjoys his two-hundred-acre ranch, filled with Western art as a wonderful retreat where he can work full-time on his books and feature film projects, and babysit grandkids as often as possible.

Also from Bestselling Author

Don Bendell

Blood Feather

ONE CRAVES BLOOD…

His name is We Wiyake, meaning "Blood Feather." He stalks the mountains and fields, searching for prey in both the native world and the white world. Killing is the one thing that makes him feel alive. But he does more than just kill—he eats his victims' hearts and leaves a blood-soaked feather on their faces.

…THE OTHER, JUSTICE.

The only person who can track Blood Feather is Joshua Strongheart, a mentor to one of the monster's victims. But Blood Feather won't be taken easily, especially since he sees Strongheart as his ultimate prey. To consume his heart would give him more power than ever. Luckily, killing a man like Joshua Strongheart is no easy task…

donbendell.com
penguin.com